CONTENTS

Crown of the Prophecy

C.A. VARIAN

Trigger Warning

There are mature themes throughout this book, and it is not intended for readers under 17 years of age.

The following themes are explored in Mate of the Phoenix: Graphic (consensual) sexual content, captivity, slavery, abduction, vulgar language, and murder.

THE WORLD OF INAS
BREQAN
EL-WAHBA
KOTOL
MONEN
ILLEVER
HARMUE SEA
HOWLING FOREST
N
MARELLA ARCH
VAEKROS

The Scorched Realm
Voiceless Mountains
Cineris
The Emerald Enclave
THE INFERNO TERRITORIES
Irriboia Sea

AEGRICIAN MOUNTAINS
AEGRICIA
FLAMECLIFF
ZORITHAE
WINDREACH
THE WORLD OF EKOTORIA
MARELLA ARCH
SPECTRE FOREST
CLAYWIND
ELDER SEA
UNDYING DESERT
DIAPOLIS
EMBERSHELL
N
WARBOTACH

PROLOGUE

VARIEL

There was an eerie orange glow over the battlefield as the sun dipped below the horizon. It was the kind of light that spoke not of endings but of things yet to come. Variel parried a blow from Joneira, her breath coming in ragged gasps as their blades clashed with the sound of ringing steel. Sweat and blood mixed in the dirt beneath their feet, the air around them thick with the heat of battle.

"Is this all you've got, oracle?" Joneira sneered, her eyes flashing with malice. "I expected more from the great Variel."

"Save your taunts." Variel's muscles strained as she pushed back against Joneira's blade. "We're not finished yet."

Around them, warriors clashed in a whirlwind of violence, blood flowing like rivers into the forest. The fierce cries of Variel's allies intertwined with the guttural war cries of the barbarians and Joneira's supporters, creating a cacophony that echoed across the land.

Dragons soared above the conflict, casting shadows on the ground with their massive wings as they battled midair. As their claws tore at scales and flesh, their roars shook the ground beneath Variel's feet. Their maws were filled with fire, scorching the ground and igniting trees in a blaze of destruction. Ash rained from the sky, coating armor and skin alike and turning the air into something almost too thick to breathe.

The weight of Variel's people's hopes and fears rested on her shoulders as she fought. She had to kill Joneira—if only to prevent Aurelia from having to do the job herself. This was the battle destiny had saved for her, a clash not just of blades but of futures.

With each swing of her sword, she channeled her anger into her attacks, determined to bring an end to the senseless conflict. But Joneira was a formidable foe. Her strikes, swift and relentless, drove Variel back, step by step.

"Your cause is lost!" A feral grin spread across Joneira's face as she pressed her advantage. "You can't win!"

Variel summoned the last of her strength as she surged forward, slashing low. "I will fight to my last breath to protect the chosen queen!"

The chaos and violence of the battle seemed to close in on them, the press of bodies and the clash of steel threatening to overwhelm Variel's senses. The scent of blood and fire filled the air, the heat of the flames licking at her skin. It was a desperate, terrifying struggle, and she knew that one wrong move could mean the end for her and her allies. The sheer intensity of the battle was palpable, a relentless force that threatened to consume them all.

In the midst of the raging battle, the ground beneath Variel and Joneira shuddered, a blast from the sea tossing them to their feet. The sudden appearance of a tear near the treeline behind Joneira caught both warriors off guard, their eyes widening as they watched the air shimmer and swirl. The earth itself seemed to recoil as if it knew what had been unleashed. All around them, the cacophony of battle continued unabated, but for a moment, they were both transfixed by the pulsating energy that threatened to consume them.

"Impossible!" Joneira gasped, her sword faltering in its relentless assault.

As Variel watched the portal, the swirling air held her transfixed. The vortex grew larger, engulfing both combatants in its depths. Their swords clattered to the ground, forgotten, as they were ripped away from the battlefield and into the unknown.

Together, Variel and Joneira hurtled through the void, the fabric of reality bending and twisting around them. The sensation of being pulled through the portal was unlike anything Variel had ever experienced, as if every muscle in her body was being stretched and compressed at once, like a piece of taffy pulled apart by invisible hands. It was like falling through a storm of shattered glass and molten stars, each fragment cutting and burning as it rushed past.

As suddenly as it had begun, the disorienting journey came to an abrupt end. With a final violent wrench, Variel and Joneira were ejected from the portal and sent hurtling through the air. They landed hard on the ground, dozens of warriors hitting the earth beside them, all gasping for breath as they struggled to make sense of their surroundings.

When she rose to her knees, the world around her was foreign, the air sharp and metallic, the sky the wrong shade of night. And she knew, with bone-deep certainty, that Ekotoria had been left behind.

CHAPTER ONE

Aurelia

With the stones tumbling from the mountains around them, Aurelia, Cristos, and Bremusa took to the sky and returned to the battlefield, Aurelia held tightly in Cristos' arms. The first sight of Flamecliff sent a chill down her spine. Ash drifted like gray snow through the broken streets, settling on toppled beams and shattered glass, a mockery of winter's peace. Much of the once-beautiful city was now a charred, smoldering ruin. The smoke billowed into the sky like the last breath of a dying world, while the moans of the wounded reverberated throughout the air, punctuated by the cries of wounded warriors searching for survivors.

Aurelia's heart ached as she surveyed the devastation. The sour scent of burnt flesh mixed with the acrid smell of scorched earth made her stomach turn. Buildings lay in shattered heaps, their once proud façades crumbled under the weight of destruction. As they ventured deeper into the chaos, the ground beneath their feet was slick with blood, staining the soles of their boots. She clenched her fists, trying not to lose her composure. Every muscle in her arms trembled with the effort, her grief clawing to escape as surely as the smoke clawed toward the heavens. It was her duty as queen to be strong for her people, but grief threatened to overwhelm her.

"By the gods," Cristos muttered, his voice catching in his throat as he surveyed the devastation around them, his wings twitching involuntarily.

With her crimson hair whipping about her face, Aurelia's blue eyes searched desperately for any signs of life among the carnage. As she stared at the scene, she wasn't sure where to begin.

"Flamecliff has suffered greatly," Bremusa began, her silver eyes somber as she gazed at the wreckage, "but we will re-build."

As they continued their search, Aurelia's gaze fell upon the crumpled form of Taryn, the warrior's sword still clutched in her hand. A choked sob escaped Aurelia's lips as she knelt beside her fallen comrade, brushing the long brown hair from Taryn's lifeless face.

"She deserved better than this." Unable to hold back any longer, a sob burst from Aurelia's throat. "They all did."

Cristos placed a hand on her shoulder, his touch grounding her. "She was a brave warrior, my love. She fought valiantly until the end."

"We've lost too much," Aurelia choked out, her vision blurred by the tears that finally spilled over. She glanced around the city as groups of warriors searched for survivors among the fallen. She knew her sister and Septima were out there some-where, perhaps with— The reality of losing her aunt hit her hard, stopping her in her tracks and wrenching her heart wide open. "First Otera and now Taryn... How many more must die before this war is over?" The thought settled like ice in her chest—war did not care for queens, sisters, or lovers. It would take until nothing remained.

"Let their sacrifices not be in vain," Bremusa said, her voice steady despite the emotion that sparked in her eyes. "We will continue our fight in their honor."

With a nod of her head, Aurelia wiped her tears away with the back of her hand. She straightened her spine, her resolve hardening as she turned to face Bremusa. "You're right, Bremusa. Our people are counting on us."

With Cristos' arm wrapped around her waist, they followed Bremusa further into the ravaged battlefield, their boots crunching over the charred earth and their eyes scanning the destruction around them.

"Aurelia!" a familiar voice called out, cutting through the thick air that lay over the battlefield. Aurelia turned to see her sister rushing toward them, her dark eyes red-rimmed with tears. Exie followed, her golden hair matted with dirt and sweat.

"Thank the gods you're alive!" Aurelia cried, embracing her sister as tightly as she could. Septima clung to her, her body shaking with sobs. When Aurelia pulled away, her hands slid up to touch her sister's face. "When the two of you flew toward the portal, I feared the worst."

As Aurelia embraced her sister, tears trailed down her dusty cheeks, but she couldn't help but feel relief. A lot of people had perished in the war, but Septima and Cristos were okay, and that was something to be happy about. Still, her heart broke for all the lost—Taryn, her aunt—who she never had a chance to know.

Looking over Septima's shoulder as her sister rubbed her back, Aurelia gazed at the destroyed portal, at the crumbling stone façade that had once encircled it like the frame of an antique mirror.

Just as she was about to pull away and tell Septima about what had transpired in the mountains—about the crimson wings that were now hiding away inside her—a violent explosion rattled through the city, and the remaining portal crumbled into the sea.

Screams erupted around them as Aurelia and Septima were forced apart and thrown several feet back. With a crash, Aurelia collided with the stone exterior of the building, sending pain exploding through her bones.

Ears ringing, she scanned her surroundings for her sister and her husband, but in the cloud of dust and ash, it was impossible to see anything.

"Cristos! Septima!"

With ash forcing her to cough and sputter, Aurelia forced herself onto her feet and did her best to assess her body for injuries. Her back ached, but her hand went instinctively to her stomach, hoping her child was unharmed inside her.

"Aurelia!" Cristos' voice cut through the ringing in her ears, drawing her toward the direction of the sea.

"Cristos! Where are you?"

The sound of heavy boots stomping met her ears a second before strong arms wrapped around her, holding her close.

"Are you hurt, love?" he asked, pulling away just enough to look into her eyes. Aside from a cut above his eyebrow, Aurelia was relieved that Cristos seemed to be unharmed.

Nodding, she rose onto her tiptoes and kissed him. "I'm okay, but where are the others?"

Before he could answer, Septima's voice sent Aurelia darting through the dusty air, Cristos on her heels. As she ran, her breath sat heavy in her chest, not knowing what she would find when she laid eyes on her friends again. But as the ash cleared, Aurelia's feet stumbled. What she saw, who she saw standing in the ashes like the phoenix she was, sent Aurelia to her knees. Otera was alive.

Scattered among the destruction, figures rose from where their lifeless bodies had lain only moments before. The air itself seemed to hum, heavy with the raw pulse of scattered magic, as if life had been borrowed from the very bones of the earth.

Tears clouded Aurelia's vision, so she closed her eyes, hoping, but not expecting, the risen to still be before her. But when she reopened them, she realized they were not figments of her imagination. The once dead Aegrician warriors were now alive.

"Otera..." With shaky legs beneath her, Aurelia stood, taking two steps closer to her aunt with Cristos' arm around her waist. "Otera... I—I don't understand."

Beside the resurrected queen, Bremusa stood with a hand on her friend. "The destruction of the portal caused its magic to disperse, bringing life to its protectors as its final act."

Trying to absorb the words, Aurelia remained silent, even as Septima and Exie moved closer to her side. Even Blaedia, whose hands searched her mate for injuries, remained silent.

Bremusa tipped her head toward the largest group of warriors, who, like Otera, had risen. "My powers tell me the portal has moved; history proves it, but with its magic diminished, it will be nearly impossible to find. Still, we must find it. The fate of the human realm depends on its protection."

The portal had been the very lifeline connecting the human realm and the fae realm for as long as the worlds existed. It allowed Aurelia and Septima, if they ever chose to, the possibility of returning home. Now, with its destruction, an unnerving cloud of scattered magic hung in the air, as if waiting to be claimed by forces unknown.

"What does this mean for our realms?" Cristos asked, his hand tightening around Aurelia's back.

Bremusa turned her eyes to Cristos, the quicksilver in them drawing Aurelia into their depths. "Both worlds are now isolated from each other. With the magic scattered, there's no telling what consequences we may face."

The words settled over Aurelia heavier than ash, a prophecy unspoken but felt—that their war had only just begun.

Chapter Two

Aurelia

Bremusa's words echoed in Aurelia's mind, their implications rattling her already fragile nerves. The weight of isolation clung to her like a vice, whispering that even the most delicate joys might shatter under the burden of fate. There had been too many changes in too short a time, but at least Otera, Taryn, and many others had risen from the ashes when the portal crumbled. That was one positive amid a sea of devastation.

As the injured were brought into infirmary tents for healing, Aurelia, Cristos, and their closest family and friends—including Otera and Blaedia—made their way to the palace near the harbor. For years, it had been Otera's home, but with her sacrifice, she was no longer the queen of Aegricia. Still, Aurelia hoped her aunt would choose to continue living there. They had only just met, and Aurelia looked forward to getting to know her mother's sister and learning from Otera how to be a ruler. Growing up in a royal family, Otera understood the responsibilities of monarchy better than anyone. Once the dust settled and the bodies were laid to rest, they needed to find a way to unite Aegricia and Norithae, just as the prophecy foretold.

"Once we get settled," Cristos said, sliding his arm around Aurelia's waist as they stepped through the massive wooden doors, "we'll send for a healer to check on you and the baby. I know you feel fine, but I would feel better knowing that everything is as it should be."

Aurelia nodded, her eyes absorbing the palace for the first time. For months, she had seen the dungeon in her dreams, witnessing Otera's neglect and abuse at the hands of the Warbotach ruler, but she had never set foot in the palace herself.

It was clear from the outside that Aegricia was a wealthy kingdom, one that had stood for centuries. The palace, constructed from a light-colored stone that looked nearly silver in the sunlight, held a majestic splendor that rivaled Diapolis in the South. Norithae's palace was beautiful, but there was something truly magical about seeing the place where her mother had been raised. Each polished arch and gleaming stair seemed to breathe with history. Yet, grief stained the grandeur, reminding Aurelia that walls alone could not keep out ruin. Although the barbarians had controlled the city of Flamecliff for months, living in the palace as if it were their own, the lack of destruction inside indicated that Uldon—or whoever he had claimed the city for—intended to stay there for a long time.

"I'm surprised there isn't more damage," Aurelia remarked, scanning the entrance as servants moved about the space, attending to their tasks as if their lives depended on it. However, the moment the doors closed behind them, every set of eyes in the room turned to face them.

"Your Majesty," an older woman said, dropping her broom and crossing the room to greet them. Otera stepped around their group, her leather garments nearly torn to shreds, and her waist-length crimson hair matted with blood and ash. The servant bowed deeply, reaching out to take Otera's hands. "I cannot tell you how relieved we are to see you."

Two more servants entered the room: a younger woman with golden hair carrying a tray of water glasses and an older man with several cloths draped over his arm.

Otera smiled, gently squeezing the servant's hand. "It's good to be home, Muriel, but there is much to do. First, I should introduce you to the new queen of Aegricia."

Aurelia's heart fluttered at Otera's words, but she remained silent. "My niece, Aurelia, has come to fulfill the prophecy. My time as queen is over."

The word "prophecy," spoken aloud in the echoing hall, seemed to ripple through the servants like a gust of wind, their eyes widening as if they, too, could feel destiny stir. With wide eyes, Muriel reached for Aurelia's hand, catching her by surprise. Although she knew it was true, acknowledging her new position was something she wasn't entirely ready for. "You'll always be queen, Otera, no matter what the crown says."

A knowing smile spread across Otera's battered face as she took one of the cloths and wiped the blood from her arms. "I'll be here to support you and Cristos, Aurelia, in whatever capacity you both need."

As exhausted as everyone was, the conversation in the foyer of the palace didn't last long. With so much left unsaid, the servants escorted Aurelia and Cristos to one of the suites in the east wing of the castle, overlooking the sea. Blaedia and Otera, along with Septima and Exie, were led to other areas within the massive structure. The group planned to reunite that evening for the funeral pyre of those who had fallen, but with the early morning sun streaming through the balcony doors of their bedroom, all Aurelia could think about was sleep.

Similar to their rooms in the Norithae palace, the suite they were brought to was vast, featuring a large four-poster bed with bright white, fluffy linens. Several pieces of gold-upholstered furniture filled the space in front of the fireplace. It was pristine and cozy, a stark contrast to the carnage outside.

Guilt swam through Aurelia's mind as she sat in such a place while so many suffered, but she knew there was only so much she could do in that moment. Her reflection in the gilded mirror by the hearth seemed almost foreign—illuminated by the firelight while others lay in shadow. Most of the civilians in Flamecliff had left the city, and the healers, who had remained at their camp during the violence, were now attending to the injured. She was just one person, and without rest, she would be no good to anyone.

"I'll prepare your bath, my love," Cristos said, kissing her on the cheek before disappearing into the bathing room.

Aurelia didn't follow; she was entranced by the view through the window and the way the sunlight made the sea sparkle like diamonds. Just as the sound of water reached her ears, a knock on the door echoed through the room, pulling her attention away from the view.

Crossing the room, she opened the door and felt relieved to see a servant standing beside a cart topped with bowls of steaming porridge, holding a stack of clean clothes in her hands. "I know it's not much, Your Majesty, but with all those who need attention, we managed to gather some clean clothes and a warm meal for the two of you. I hope this can sustain you for a little while."

Aurelia smiled and reached out to take the clothes from the young woman's hands. "This is perfect, Miss..."

"Kassandra," the girl said, dipping into a curtsy. Although it was difficult to tell with fae, Aurelia guessed she couldn't be much older than a teenager.

"It's nice to meet you, Kassandra."

Cristos called her name, drawing Aurelia's attention briefly. "My husband and I will be getting cleaned up and trying to rest, but if you could see to it that a healer finds me at dinner time, I would appreciate it."

Kassandra replied with a nod and another smile before bringing their food into the room and then disappearing down the corridor.

Closing the door, Aurelia set the clothes down on the bed and walked into the bathing room, her heavy heart fluttering at the sight of her husband removing his leathers, his massive wings stretching at his sides. He was magnificent.

"A servant, Kassandra, brought a warm meal and clean clothes for us," she said.

Cristos turned to face her, licking his lips as she unbuckled her leathers and let them drop to the floor. "And the healer? Are they sending someone?"

Kicking his soiled clothes to the side, he closed the distance between them and slid his hand against her still-flat stomach, as if he could already feel their child kicking. Given everything they had been through, their unborn child was a beacon of hope for the future.

As Cristos leaned down to kiss her stomach, she threaded her fingers into his thick black hair. "I asked her to send someone this evening. We both need rest, and there are so many who need a healer more than I do right now."

With a nod, he wrapped his arm around her waist, guiding her to the steaming bathtub. "Then let's get you cleaned up and into bed."

Pounding on the door reverberated through the chamber, jolting Aurelia from a deep sleep. Cristos, her steadfast companion, slipped out of bed with a swiftness that revealed his readiness, answering the intrusion before she could fully process the disturbance. Muffled voices and purposeful footsteps followed, weaving an unspoken narrative of urgency. A moment later, Cristos returned to her side, accompanied by an elderly Aegrician woman with long, elegantly braided silver hair.

With a warm smile that accentuated the crinkles around her eyes, the elder introduced herself. "Good morning, Your Majesty. My name is Cordelia. Would it be alright if I check on you and your baby?"

Aurelia, still grappling with the abrupt awakening, nodded with a hint of confusion. "Yes, but I feel fine."

Cordelia approached, placing her bag on the bedside table, and withdrew a device to listen to Aurelia's heartbeat. The air hung heavy with unspoken concern as Cordelia began her examination. "Your husband explained the transformation you went through when the portal fell."

A surge of memories cascaded through Aurelia's mind—the chaos in the mountains and the searing sensation of wings bursting forth from her back. She shuddered, seeking reassurance. "Do you think it caused harm to our child?" Her gaze flicked to Cristos, noting the worry etched on his face.

The silence that followed was laden with anticipation. After feeling Aurelia's stomach and prompting her to turn onto her side, Cordelia ran her ice-cold hands up Aurelia's back, shifting her tunic aside for a more thorough examination. "Your skin looks as it should, Your Majesty—just like any of our warriors. And your child is showing no signs of distress." Still, Cordelia's eyes lingered on Aurelia's back for a moment too long, as though some secret lay beneath the skin that even she could not identify.

Letting out a breath that Aurelia felt in her own chest, Cristos drew closer, taking Aurelia's hand and kissing her knuckles. "Well, that's good news, love."

Cordelia hummed her agreement from her position at Aurelia's back. "Indeed, it is. However, I want to see you rest for a few days—just to be sure."

An immediate protest formed on Aurelia's lips, a testament to her resilience and sense of duty. Before she could voice her objections, Cristos shook his head, offering gentle reassurance. "I know we all have a lot to do right now, love, but everyone is here to help. It's not worth risking harm to you or our child if you overdo it."

While Cristos's words made sense, an internal struggle began to brew within Aurelia. As queen, she felt an intrinsic responsibility to be at the forefront, actively participating in the challenges facing their kingdom. The idea of lying in bed while her people toiled and suffered seemed inconceivable. Though she yearned to argue, the weight of Cristos's gaze and the healer's advice compelled her compliance. She reclined on the bed and turned her attention to Cordelia. "For how long? Is there anything I should be aware of? Any warning signs?"

Cordelia's lips curled into a small smile as she tidied up her tools. "Well... I've never seen a transformation like this before. Even in the lore, this doesn't happen—not the way it happened to you—so I can't provide an exact answer. Still, I think if you rest through tomorrow and don't experience any bleeding or pain, you should be fine—both you and the baby."

Bidding Aurelia and Cristos farewell, Cordelia left their quarters with a promise to return the following day. Aurelia huffed out a breath, frustration making her nerves antsy at the thought of not leaving their rooms for two days. Part of her wanted to escape, at least to go down to the kitchens and get to know the people working in her palace. Just as she was about to climb out of bed, another knock sounded at the door. Only a moment later, her sister walked in.

Relief and dread mingled in Aurelia's chest—her sister's presence was a balm, yet every knock on the door seemed to carry the weight of fate demanding to be heard.

Chapter Three

Kason

Although the fight had destroyed much of Flamecliff, leaving rubble along the mountain pass that separated Aegricia and Norithae, the Singing Lantern tavern emerged virtually unscathed. Amid the devastation, it remained a refuge, offering hot meals and warm beds to those who had nowhere else to go. The walls were infused with the scents of smoke and old whiskey, a cocoon of familiarity standing defiantly against the encroaching ruin outside.

Bruised and battered from the battle, Kason and Holera slid into a booth at the back of the room and ordered a decanter of whiskey. The atmosphere in the city was tense, yet their people were resilient, just as phoenixes were meant to be.

Sitting next to him, Holera's silver hair was caked with soot, and the smudges across her face blended with the battle paint she often applied before a fight.

"Do you want to head upstairs?" he asked, wrapping his fingers around her slender hand. He could sense how frayed her nerves were after the day's extremes. The thought of potentially losing her made him want to hold her tighter—to protect her from all harm. The memory of her wings faltering in battle had nearly torn him apart, leaving him with a fear he dared not express.

They still had too many dreams waiting to manifest—dreams of retiring from the fight and starting a family. However, their kingdom had faced near-constant threats since they had met, and the timing had never felt right. Soon, he promised himself. They would retire to their cottage tucked away in the mountains, and he would keep her in bed for days, worshiping her as she deserved. He envisioned a hearth fire instead of battle flames, imagining her laughter echoing through rooms untouched by war—a dream so fragile it almost hurt to contemplate.

Exhaustion weighed down Holera's lashes, and she nodded. "Yes. I feel if I don't get these leathers off soon, they may become permanently affixed to my skin." Even her usual spark was dimmed; the fire in her violet eyes was shuttered beneath a fatigue carved by years of relentless battle.

Kason chuckled, standing up and positioning himself to lift her from the chair. If she were too weak to walk, he fully intended to carry her. "Well, we can't have that, my stunning warrior. I won't tolerate anything blocking me from tasting every inch of your skin."

Even in her half-asleep state, she grinned, not protesting as he lifted her into his arms. With his other hand, he grabbed the decanter of whiskey and carried them both up the stairs.

For as long as they had been together, there was one room at the tavern that was Kason's whenever he needed it. He hadn't used it much over the past year. As an emissary for Aegricia, he had traveled for the queen. He hadn't spent enough time in Flamecliff to warrant buying a home there. He could have taken a room in the palace, but a life as an upper-class male was not in his blood. He had been born and raised in the Aegrician outlands, deep within the mountains, while Holera had grown up in the rural plains of Western Aegricia. Neither of them relished the thought of living in the city or being under constant scrutiny. Staying in the palace would mean being watched by hundreds of staff and guards, which was why they had never chosen to stay at the Aegrician palace; instead, they had opted for the Diapolisian palace when there was no other easy option.

Climbing up the wooden stairs to the second level, Kason set the decanter down on the small table in the corridor and fished the key from his pocket. Holera was already asleep in his arms, so once they were inside the room, he gently laid her on the settee. With tender hands, he removed her boots and leathers, careful not to wake her. He knew she would want to clean up before bed, so he had no issue tending to her while she slumbered. The battle had drained both of them, but as a phoenix shifter, her body underwent a metamorphosis he could never experience.

Once his beautiful mate was stripped bare, he filled a wash basin with warm water and used a cloth to clean the worst of the grime from her before tucking her into bed.

After washing himself as best as he could, he climbed into bed beside her, pulling her smaller body against his chest where she fit perfectly—like a missing piece of him that made him whole again. Outside the windows, destruction lay every-where, but for the moment, their enemies were gone, and the healers were tending to the sick and injured. All that remained for him and his warrior mate was to rest so they could face another day. They knew their kingdom would soon need them again, so they needed to take advantage of this moment of peace.

Waking the next morning, Kason pulled Holera close, wishing they could stay in bed all day. But he knew they couldn't. Duty called to them, even if they couldn't hear it with their ears. "Just a little longer, and we can hide away," he repeated to himself as they dressed and left the inn to head back to the palace.

Tents lined the treeline on both sides of the main road leading toward the harbor, not only infirmary tents but also temporary shelters for those whose homes had been affected by the war. It was a temporary solution, but it was necessary.

Taking Holera by the hand, Kason nodded at the guards by the front gates as they swung open. "We're going to have to talk about finding the missing portal," Holera said, her violet eyes shining in the rising sun. "And who's going out to look for it."

Kason nodded, pulling her to his side so he could kiss the top of her head. "Is that something you want us to do? Do you want to be part of that team?"

Although he asked the question, he already knew the answer. As long as they went together, he didn't care. They were always a team, no matter where they went.

She shot him a side-eye, her feisty attitude making him chuckle. "Point taken."

As they opened the palace's front doors, they were met with a chaotic scene. Servants and guards bustled around the main entrance and corridor. "You're the best diplomat for this kingdom I know, my love," Holera said, squeezing his hand. "If anyone can get to the bottom of where the portal's magic went, it's you."

Kason grinned at his mate's compliment, fully aware that she meant it, but he also knew she had her own agenda. "You're just saying that because you want to go."

The smirk that lifted the corner of Holera's full lips made his desire stir, but he pushed it aside as they turned down the corridor into the eastern wing, heading toward the war room. This was the meeting space where Queen Otera had spent a lot of her time. She was no longer queen, but Kason didn't doubt that Aurelia would continue this tradition. That was why he was surprised when they entered the large room and found Otera, Blaedia, Bremusa, and Cristos there, but no Aurelia.

When Kason and Holera stepped into the room, every head turned to look at them. "Oh, Kason and Holera," Blaedia said, dipping her head in greeting. It was the friendliest expression the usually severe general ever displayed. Blaedia may have been stunning, but she rarely smiled. Her mate, Otera, beamed as Kason and Holera approached her, with Holera pulling her into a hug. Even his mate tended to be serious and didn't often show her emotions, but after witnessing their queen's death and the rise from the ashes, all their foundations had been shaken to the core.

"Where's Aurelia?" Holera asked, clearly wondering the same thing as Kason.

Cristos smiled and stepped around the table to hug Holera. "My stubborn mate is begrudgingly on bed rest for a few days. She's okay, but the healer wants to ensure that our child in her womb suffers no ill effects after everything Aurelia went through yesterday."

Kason gripped Cristos' forearm, dipping his chin and smiling. "I'm sure they're both fine, but it's good that the healer is forcing her to rest. The kingdom will still be here, as will the work."

Nodding, Cristos turned to look down at the map spread out on the table. "There will be a lot to do for a very long time." The weight of his words pressed upon them like the map itself—lines and borders that signified responsibility, not rest.

CHAPTER FOUR

AURELIA

The walls seemed to close in around Aurelia as she lay in bed, staring at the flickering flames in the fireplace while the rest of her kingdom dealt with the aftermath of the war. The thought of everyone else managing the decisions—the work, the grief—while she remained warm in her bed filled her with guilt. Each muffled voice from the corridor pressed against her conscience, reminding her that rest was a luxury others could not afford. She understood why the healer wanted her to rest for a few days; her child was worth it, but that didn't ease her mind.

Around midday, the door to her chambers opened, rousing her from her nap. She expected to see a servant bringing in a tray of food or perhaps the healer checking in on her, but it was Cristos who walked in, carrying a tray of food. For a moment, memories of their first meeting flooded her mind—not when he walked alongside the cart carrying her after the barbarians had captured her and her friends, but when he entered the dungeon to bring her and the others food. It felt like years since they'd met, even though it had only been months. The handsome winged stranger who had rescued her from the barbarians had become everything to her, bringing a smile to her face as he entered the room. The memory of chains still lingered in her dreams, but the weight of his arms around her now was proof that captivity had given way to love.

"Did I wake you, my love?" he asked, setting the tray down on the table and crossing the room to kiss her, the scent of roasted meat and vegetables making her stomach rumble.

As the kiss lingered, the aroma of their lunch was replaced by Cristos' sandalwood and spice scent, drawing a groan from her chest. It was one more thing about him that comforted her, even in her most tumultuous moments.

When he pulled away, she shook her head, a smile lifting the corners of her lips. "I was just dozing. You didn't wake me."

Cristos smiled back, cupping her cheek in his palm. "I hope you've been getting lots of rest...and that you're hungry. Otera had the cook, Ellisar, prepare a lunch with plenty of fresh vegetables for you."

Taking her hand, Cristos helped Aurelia out of bed. Her body ached from her ordeal, but it was nothing she couldn't manage. "You'll have to thank her for me. Will you be meeting again this afternoon? How did it go this morning? Did you see my sister?"

Pulling out a chair for her, Cristos chuckled at how quickly the questions left her mouth, unable to answer one before she asked another. "We met this morning and discussed what needs to be done in this first stage and delegated tasks so we won't need to meet again tonight. I understand that Exie and Septima have been in town since early this morning helping with cleanup, so I haven't seen them yet today."

Taking a bite of her food, Aurelia closed her eyes, willing the nausea building in her chest to dissipate. When she opened her eyes, she gazed out the window at the sea, amazed at how the sun made the surface sparkle like diamonds. The portal, once a massive archway of jagged stones eroded by the sea, was no longer there; its remains had sunk to the depths, where they would never be seen again. But the essence of the portal itself, the magic that had allowed Aurelia and her sister to enter Aegricia all those months ago, was gone. Its absence left a silence more haunting than battle cries—a gap in the world that seemed to echo inside her chest.

Her expression turning pensive, she returned her gaze to her husband, finding him watching her. "And the portal...when will the search for it begin?"

Before Cristos could respond, a knock sounded at the door, drawing their attention. Cristos stood from the table and crossed the room, and Aurelia's heart leaped when he opened the door to reveal her sister and Exie standing there. She hadn't realized how much she needed to see Septima until she was standing in front of her, dirty clothes and exhaustion evident, but safe.

"Sissy!" Aurelia exclaimed, a smile spreading across her face that mirrored the expression on Septima's face. She moved to stand, but Septima was at her side in an instant, the speed of her movement catching Aurelia by surprise. Still at the door, Exie and Cristos chatted.

Septima lowered herself into Cristos' chair, leaned forward, and pulled Aurelia into a hug. "It seems the portal's collapse changed more than just you," she said, raising an eyebrow. It didn't take long for Aurelia to notice that Septima's once perfectly rounded ears had begun to taper at the top. Aurelia's mouth fell open, her hands bracing on Septima's shoulders as she searched her sister's face. The faint point of Septima's ears glimmered like a newly unveiled secret, marking a change that bound them even closer to this realm.

"The magic... it turned you fae?" Aurelia asked, her eyes wide with surprise.

Septima's smile widened. "I saw a healer this morning. They aren't sure how much it will affect me—like if it will lengthen my lifespan—but I've definitely started developing some fae traits! I'm faster, and my wounds have already healed."

For a moment, Aurelia didn't respond, relief flooding through her even as questions lingered. She hadn't even had time to consider whether the new magic in her veins would affect her own lifespan. "That's amazing, Septima."

"That's not all," Septima said, gazing out the window before returning her deep brown eyes to Aurelia. "Bremusa said if we can find the portal, we may be able to cross it. We could see Amadeus again...and Father."

The thought had never seemed possible to Aurelia. To prevent Septima from being forced to marry a man, she had agreed to never see her father and brother again. At the time, it felt like the right decision, but it didn't numb the aching hole in her chest created by the loss of those she loved. Even with everything she had been going through over the past few months—new husband, a child on the way, and a found family—she still missed them. "But the treaty—"

Septima shook her head, but it was Exie who spoke as she and Cristos approached the table. "The treaty was with Aegricia and the portal off its coast. The new portal, wherever it is, will require a new treaty. Diplomats from our realm will have to venture into the human realm and work with their kingdoms to create a new agreement."

The thought unsettled Aurelia—her homeland had been a cage. Yet, the idea of strangers negotiating its fate without her present made her blood run cold. The prospect should have relieved some of the tension in her chest, but it only tightened it further. "But I won't be able to go." Aurelia's gaze flicked up toward Cristos, as if seeking permission, even though she knew he would never stand in her way, especially not when there was a chance to see her family. He held her gaze but remained silent. "The baby... the kingdom. I'm needed here."

With the weight of her decisions dragging her down, Aurelia turned her gaze back to the endless blue outside the window, a tear trailing down her cheek as disappointment sliced through her heart. "You must tell my father and brother how much I love them when you see them, Sissy. Tell them how sorry I am for abandoning them."

Lowering himself onto one knee, Cristos slid his fingers along her cheek, wiping away her tears as he nudged her to look at him. "Otera can run the kingdom while you're away, my love. Many people are capable of taking care of Aegricia while we're gone. I won't let you miss this opportunity for closure, and I won't let anything happen to you or our child."

After they ate lunch, Septima and Exie left to return to the cleanup effort outside the palace. Cristos had another meeting scheduled with Otera and some others, but he sent a message asking them to meet in his and Aurelia's chambers instead of the war room. Aurelia, although on bedrest, was determined to be involved in the decision-making regarding the post-war world. As the new Aegrician queen—one who didn't feel qualified at all—she wanted to learn from her aunt, whom she had thought she'd lost just a day earlier. Important decisions needed to be made, and she didn't want to miss the opportunity to contribute.

While Cristos prepared their private dining area for the meeting, Aurelia slipped into the bathing room to freshen up and put on a tunic and trousers. When she walked back out, Otera, Blaedia, and Bremusa were already there, looking over a large map spread out on the table.

"Otera!" Seeing her aunt, who looked so much like her mother, tore at Aurelia's heart. The former queen truly was a phoenix. Otera smiled and wrapped her arms around her niece.

"Aren't you supposed to be resting?" Otera asked.

Looking up at them, Cristos smirked. "Your niece doesn't know the meaning of the word."

Aurelia scoffed, pulling away from Otera and sitting at the table. "I can rest and still be part of the discussions. Spending more time alone when so much needs to be done may drive me insane."

It wasn't until after the words left her mouth that she realized how insensitive it was to complain about such things after Otera had spent months in the dungeon below her own palace. However, Otera seemed unfazed. She rubbed Aurelia's shoulder, then moved to stand beside Cristos, leaving a space for Aurelia to see the map between them.

"We're sending scouts to the south and west," Cristos said, tracing a path toward Diapolis and the forested area north of Warbotach. "If there's a portal there, the scouts should be able to sense it."

Bremusa nodded, her long black hair pulled back in a braid slipping over her shoulder as she twisted her head to look at him. After having seen her as an elderly woman with a hunched back in many visions, it was strange for Aurelia to see Bremusa in her true form. Her shifting ability was astounding. As a full-blooded elemental centuries old, Bremusa looked no older than twenty-five. However, her quicksilver eyes spoke of an ancient wisdom that Aurelia could only dream of.

"I will consult the shadow glass," Bremusa said, pulling a second map from underneath the first and placing it on top. "My intuition tells me it may not be on the continent at all—that someone may have seen our hand before we played it and could take the magic that dispersed to them. I must admit, even I wasn't prepared for what would happen when we destroyed the crown. I believe the portal has moved. I sense its power remains in our world, but never before have I lived in a world without it. If a portal to the human world is truly gone, how would any of us ever know?"

Her words seemed to carry the weight of prophecy, each syllable falling like ash—truths that even time itself seemed reluctant to reveal.

Aurelia felt her mouth go dry, her heart sinking as her sister's hope had just lifted it from despair. "So, you're saying we may search for it forever and never find it?" Aurelia asked, the possibility of having no way back to the other half of her family making her stomach turn. "It may no longer exist?"

When Cristos' eyes met hers, Aurelia knew he understood the unspoken fear behind her words. As long as there was a portal, the option to see her father and brother remained. But if the portal were gone, she would never see them again. The thought hollowed her chest, filling her with grief not of losses past, but of futures stolen before they could be lived.

CHAPTER FIVE

Variel

Variel's eyes fluttered open, her chest heaving with labored breaths. The cold dampness of the forest floor seeped through her clothes, sending shivers down her spine. Panic set in as the unfamiliar forest seemed to close in around her. The air was heavy and suffocating, as though the trees themselves leaned closer to listen to her fear.

"Where are we?" she muttered under her breath, struggling to sit up. Her keen wolf senses picked up the distant groans and moans of injured warriors, both friends and foes, scattered throughout the trees. The stench of blood and sweat filled the air, but there was no sign of Joneira, although Variel instinctively knew they had ended up in the same place. The mixed scents clung to her like ghosts, as if the earth itself mourned the bodies it could not yet bury.

The forest was dense and mountainous, with towering ancient trees casting shadows upon the moss-covered ground. Although the branches swayed gently, thickets of brambles grew abundantly, their thorns gleaming with malice. Even though Variel knew they weren't in Spectre Forest, her instincts warned her of dangers lurking in the shadows.

"Thalius, wake up," Variel whispered urgently as she shook the shoulder of the Norithaean warrior beside her. There were both Norithaean and Aegrician warriors in the chaotic scene around them, but there were nearly twice as many enemy soldiers. Variel knew she needed to get her allies hidden away before the enemies woke and launched another attack. There would be time to fight each other later, but first, they needed to figure out where they were and create a camp for shelter. Once everyone was rested and healed, they could locate the portal and return to their world.

Jolting awake, Thalius' eyes flickered open, confusion etched across his face. A wound on his forearm had already begun to stitch closed, indicating it had been there for at least a day. Even with the fae resilience knitting his flesh, the pallor of his skin told her that time was running thin.

"Where are we?" He scanned their surroundings, uncertainty clouding his handsome features.

Variel shrugged, helping him to his feet. "I'm not sure, but we're no longer in Ekotoria. We need to wake our allies and get away from this site before our enemies awaken. Many people need healing before they can fight again."

The sun dipped below the horizon as Variel and the other warriors found a clearing in the lush forest, the cool mountain air indicating that the night would only get colder. They had been hiking for hours, narrowly escaping their enemies before realizing they had been transported to another place.

Only Variel and one other member of her group could create invisibility wards, so they set to work erecting a barrier around the campsite while the others pitched the few tents they had and built a fire. There was not nearly enough shelter for everyone to have their own tent, as not everyone had brought camping gear while they fought. However, they intended to share and make the best of what they had. A few warriors had ventured out to hunt just before darkness fell over the camp, but the unknown terrain and lurking enemies made that a risky endeavor.

As the wards enveloped them in a protective bubble, the air inside warmed, and the sounds of the forest diminished. With the protective ward in place, their enemies could pass by their camp without seeing them. Still, Variel felt the air pressing against her like glass—thin, fragile, just a tremor away from collapse.

The hunters returned to the camp just as Variel finished bandaging the last of the injured warriors. Their wounds were healing quickly thanks to their fae blood, but she wanted to ensure they wouldn't get an infection while out in the wilderness.

Morwen, an Aegrician warrior, walked across the camp with a deer slung over her shoulder and dropped her kill on the ground by the fire. Pulling her blade from a sheath at her thigh, she crouched down to begin breaking down the animal.

"Do you need some help?" Variel asked, taking her own dagger and slicing into the deer's stomach to clean out its bowels as Morwen skinned and filleted the animal.

Working together, they quickly prepared the meat for the fire, filling the campsite with an aroma that made Variel's stomach growl. Her wolf senses urged her to devour the flesh while it was still raw. If she had been in wolf form, she would have done just that. The beast inside her stirred, restless and hungry, reminding her that survival often came at the cost of teeth and blood.

While the deer cooked over the open fire, Variel slipped back inside the tent she would share with four other warriors. She removed her clothing and washed it in a basin of water they had filled from a nearby stream. After hanging her damp clothes on a hook, she slipped out the back of the tent, shifting into a massive black wolf and slipping into the shadows.

In her wolf form, Variel was able to blend into the darkness and explore her surroundings in relative safety. She longed to bathe in the stream and wash away the remnants of battle from her skin. No matter what dangers lurked in the forest, she felt confident she was one of the most formidable creatures there.

The distant murmur of the campfire faded behind her as the forest enveloped Variel in a symphony of nocturnal sounds—the hooting of owls, the chirping of crickets, and the distant howling of other creatures echoing through the trees. Under the veil of the moonlit night, her black fur glistened as she moved silently through the dense forest, her senses heightened in her lupine form. A cool breeze rustled through the leaves, carrying the scent of pine and earth, guiding her through the darkness. In her wolf form, navigating the rugged terrain was no challenge at all.

As she padded along the narrow trails, her keen eyes caught subtle movements in the underbrush where creatures stirred in the shadows. Heading back toward the direction they had traveled earlier that day, the stream beckoned to her with its gentle flow, a soothing melody that would help cleanse the traces of conflict from her fur.

Upon reaching the water's edge, Variel dipped her snout into the cool liquid, reveling in the refreshing sensation that washed away the signs of battle from her face. Moonlight danced on the rippling water, casting a silver glow on her sleek, obsidian form.

As Variel lingered by the stream, her lupine senses attuned to her surroundings, an unsettling realization began to form. The usual magical aura she had come to expect—the presence of mythical creatures, portals, even the faint echoes of sprites—was conspicuously absent. Her large ears twitched as she strained to catch the distant whispers of magical wings, but the night remained still, devoid of any enchantment.

Confusion furrowed her brow, and unease settled in her stomach as the realization she had been trying to deny pressed upon her: this was not a magical continent. Though there were other realms in the magical world of Ekotoria—many of which Variel had never visited—this place was not magical at all. Wherever the portal had dropped them, they had been left to fend for themselves in the human realm. The weight of this revelation pounded through her like a second heartbeat. It was clear now that this land was silent because it lacked the magic that once sang. The thought that there might be no way for them to return home filled Variel with a sense of dread.

CHAPTER SIX

BREMUSA

Moonlight glittered off the Elder Sea as Bremusa, in her golden phoenix form, soared low over the remnants of the portal. She searched for any trace of it, but it was simply gone. The portal was missing, along with the magic that had once surrounded it. The ships that had raced toward the portal in a last-ditch effort during the final hour of the war were also lost; they either lay at the bottom of the icy blue waters or drifted somewhere in the realm, poised to cause chaos another day. However, Bremusa was not focused on those lost enemies at that moment. Her priority was to locate the missing portal and return it to its rightful home in Aegricia, restoring balance between the worlds. There was no telling how the absence of the portal could affect their realm, and Bremusa wasn't eager to find out.

Below her, the sea churned like a wounded beast, its dark waves swallowing every trace of what had once connected their realms. Though her feathers bristled in the wind and she inhaled deeply, seeking the pull of the magic, it was of no use. The portal, wherever it was, remained out of her reach.

Circling around a bottomless whirlpool, she summoned the power of the water deep within herself, forcing it out with a thunderous beat of her massive wings. At her command, the waters stilled, revealing remnants of a ship—broken planks and torn strips of a sail—rising to the surface. The wreckage bobbed like corpses in a graveyard of water, silent testimony to the futility of greed. The Warbotach, who had raced for the portal, were gone, swallowed by the very power they had bled so many to control.

Leaving the wreckage behind, Bremusa flew against the wind over the snow-covered peaks of the Aegrician mountains. For centuries, she had made this journey, gaining knowledge from the Shadow Glass—an enchanted mirror passed down from her mother, a powerful elemental even stronger than she. The Shadow Glass enhanced her ability to foresee what others could not and to provide prophecies that could shape their world. The last prophecy she had received spoke of Aurelia, Messalina's daughter, who was predicted to return to Aegricia, take the crown, and unite northern Ekotoria, bringing peace to their continent once more.

Just the thought of Messalina sent a sharp pain through Bremusa's chest. Her laughter still echoed in her memory, haunting Bremusa more deeply than any battlefield cry ever had. Messalina had been her best friend, Otera's sister, and Aurelia's mother. She had been chased out of her kingdom and slaughtered by the exiled queen, Joneira, who had stolen the throne during Messalina's grandmother's reign. It was Bremusa's prophecy that had sent Messalina into the human realm to find her mate, and not a day had gone by without Bremusa doubting her decision. Messalina had found her mate and given birth to two children, but she was murdered before her children reached adulthood. Messalina's life had ended tragically, just like that of her mother and grandmother, leaving Otera to rule alone from the throne while grieving for her entire family.

The entrance of the cave where the Shadow Glass lay hidden came into view as Bremusa dove past the tallest ridge. The magic protecting the entrance rippled as she landed just inside, shifting back into her fae form. The moment she took a step into the cavern, unease prickled her skin like a thousand tiny spiders, the air stinging with sour magic. It was the kind of wrongness that made the heart falter, as though even the stone remembered what had been stolen.

Slowing her steps, Bremusa slid her dagger out of its sheath at her thigh, the blade gleaming in the ethereal moonlight. The air in the cave was frigid, sending her breath into dancing plumes in front of her. She listened for footsteps, but the mountains were silent, aside from the distant taps of a waterfall that had thawed in the cold. Bremusa's instincts told her that no one was there. Still, when she peeled back the final ward and stepped into the interior chamber where the Shadow Glass was kept, she realized someone had been there, and they had taken something incredibly valuable.

The metal clattered against the stone floor as Bremusa's dagger slipped from her trembling hand, her breath catching at the sight of the empty cave wall. For as long as she could remember, a large mirror had leaned against the jagged stone surface. Its intricately carved frame was covered with vines that had somehow thrived in the darkness. They wove through every crack and crevice, as though the mirror's power gave them life in a place where the sun could not reach. Now, with the Shadow Glass ripped away, the vines hung broken and dying. The once palpable thrum of power that filled the air was gone, and silence enveloped the chamber like a tomb, stripping it of breath and leaving her adrift in a void where prophecy once flourished. Even Bremusa's mind, usually brimming with the knowledge the mirror wished to share, was now unbearably quiet.

Her heart echoed a slow, thunderous beat, rattling her bones and threatening to drop her to her knees. As her emotions warred within her, she felt uncertain about what to do first, where to look, or whom to tell. All she could do was step forward and trace the stone that had once been hidden by the mirror, its color bleached from years of protection. It felt cold, lifeless, and ordinary, unworthy of the greatness that had once stood before it.

Shaking her head, she backed away, scanning the empty chamber. She inhaled deeply, hoping to catch a hint of who had been there before her, but the intruder had covered their tracks well. There was no trace of their scent, only remnants of an unrecognizable magic, alongside the brine of the sea and the fragrant pine of the distant Spectre Forest.

Several moments passed as Bremusa stared at the vacant wall until a bat flitted by, breaking her trance and prompting her into action. She slid her dagger back into its sheath, crouched down, and pressed her hands to the ground, closing her eyes. She focused her mind on the energy around her—the particles in the air—willing her senses to reveal any trace left by the thief. A swirling vision formed in her mind.

Wood creaked, rocking and swaying in the churning sea as boots hurried overhead, creating a kind of cadence. The craft groaned, as though it might burst at any moment under nature's fury. Her mind cleared. Although the vision was brief, it imparted one essential piece of information: wherever the Shadow Glass was, it wouldn't be easy to find. The rhythm of the boots on the groaning deck lingered in her mind, a promise of storms yet to come.

With her stomach churning from the realization and acid burning in her throat, Bremusa stood up on shaky legs and glanced back at the spot where the enchanted artifact had once been, its absence a stark reminder of all they had to lose.

The return flight to the palace reminded Bremusa of the night she had sent Messalina Lumino away more than two decades earlier. That night, the Shadow Glass was still in its rightful place, but someone had broken into the cave, abused its power to uncover its secrets, and forced their way into the palace to kill the queen. Now, the stakes were just as high, even though the queen was asleep and relatively safe in her bed. With the Shadow Glass potentially in enemy hands, everyone was at risk.

As she circled around the highest peak and descended into the mountain pass, Bremusa landed just inside the terrace of her north-facing tower. She wasted no time leaving her rooms and made her way down several floors of stairs across the palace to the wing where she would find Aurelia and Cristos.

"You," she called, raising her hand to signal one of the guards standing at attention near the end of the corridor by Otera

and Blaedia's rooms. The young male guard, Lukas, turned his head and nodded in acknowledgment. "Summon the former queen and the general to your new queen's rooms. It's urgent."

Her voice trembled under the weight of centuries, for she knew all too well that when prophecies went missing, entire realms could unravel.

CHAPTER SEVEN

AURELIA

A chaotic pounding at the door jolted Aurelia from a fitful sleep, the door swinging open before she had even rolled out of bed. Each blow echoed like thunder in her chest, pulling her from uneasy dreams into a waking storm. Beside her, Cristos jumped out of bed and grabbed his sword from against the wall. Muffled voices reached her ears just moments before Bremusa appeared around the corner, her dark hair a mess and her eyes wild.

"Your Majesties—I—" the guard who had been stationed at their door gasped, running up behind Bremusa, his face flushed, likely from arguing with the elemental before she burst in.

Cristos raised his hand. "It's okay, Pelius. If Otera or the others arrive, please let them through."

With a quick nod, the young guard turned and left the room.

Once he was gone, Aurelia and Cristos turned their attention back to Bremusa, who looked as if she hadn't blinked. "What's wrong, Bremusa? Did something happen?" Aurelia asked, pushing the blanket off as she swung her legs over the side of the bed.

"Otera," Bremusa replied.

"No," she added quickly, stepping forward to place her hand on Aurelia's forearm, halting her movements. "Otera is fine. I've summoned her and Blaedia."

As though their names had been called upon the wind, the former queen and the general entered the room, Otera still fastening the laces on her tunic. "What's happened?" she asked, concern etched on her face.

Every eye in the room turned to Bremusa, who clearly had something urgent to share. Aurelia's heartbeat slowed, but not to a calming rhythm; it was an uncertain pace, as if unsure whether it was safe to make a sound.

Bremusa glanced over her shoulder to ensure the door to the suite was closed before fixing her gaze on her new queen. "We face more than mere uncertainty. The Shadow Glass—our compass through chaos—has vanished."

The words hung heavily in the room, a thick silence spreading as if even the flames in the hearth dared not crackle.

After a pregnant pause, Otera finally spoke. "Missing?"

"Without it, the balance we fight for remains a dream caught in morning's light," Bremusa explained, her spine straightening with resolve. "If it falls into hands that crave not restoration but ruin, our kingdom will bleed shadows until none remember the sun."

Her voice was solemn, each syllable pressing on Aurelia's shoulders like unseen chains.

"Then we must find it," Otera declared, her words slicing through the tension. "For Aegricia, and for the realms that share its fate."

Bremusa's eyes went distant, as if she were seeing something beyond the present. "Through a veil of mist and time, the gateway beckons. It is not just a path, but a promise—to heal the fractures splintering our lands."

"But where, Bremusa? Where do we search?" Even with her royal poise, Otera's face grew flustered.

Instead of responding verbally, Bremusa reached out, placing her hand gently on Otera's cheek. Closing her eyes, Otera settled into the touch. Aurelia quickly realized what was happening: Bremusa was sharing a vision with her aunt.

The vision was brief, lasting only a minute. When it was over, Otera opened her blue eyes, confusion creasing her brow. "A ship? To where?"

"Inferno Territories?" Cristos interjected as he carried two chairs from near the table and placed them closer to the bed for the others to sit. Otera lowered herself into one chair, while Blaedia opted to stand by her side, resting a hand on her mate's shoulder.

Otera and Bremusa nodded in agreement. "There are only so many continents in the fae world that require a ship to reach… well, known continents, anyway," Bremusa clarified.

"I don't understand how anyone could have gotten past the wards protecting it. They should have been impenetrable," Otera remarked, pulling her long crimson hair over her shoulder to braid it.

Bremusa nodded. "They should have been. I reinforced them myself." It was clear to Aurelia that, although she didn't know Bremusa well, the elemental was flustered, almost speechless about the turn of events. "All I can conclude is that the destruction of the portal affected them in some way, allowing someone to slip past them in the chaos and manage to smuggle it out."

Though Aurelia had been thrust into the position of queen in the fae realm, she felt like a newborn, learning from those around her. She didn't know what questions to ask or what dangers could befall them, nor did she understand what powers the Shadow Glass held. This realization stung—how could she be queen when she still felt like a child, peering at the world through someone else's eyes? "I would like to see your vision," she said, breaking the silence.

Flashbacks of the vision still lingered in Aurelia's mind as she nibbled on her breakfast a short time later, still unsure of what they were searching for. For all they knew, the ship in the vision Bremusa had shared with her might have gone straight to the bottom of the Elder Sea when the portal exploded, rather than sailing west toward the Inferno Territories. There was even a chance that the Shadow Glass had made it onto a ship headed for Diapolis, prompting the unsettling thought that King Ailani might have betrayed them. However, no one wanted to entertain that possibility. Still, it was something Holera and Kason would have to explore.

With the sea now silent beneath Bremusa's powerful influence, Aurelia didn't believe the artifact had gone down with any of the doomed ships. Yet she wasn't prepared to completely rule it out. If she were honest with herself, the artifact could be anywhere. With their departure within the hour, they had no clear target to pursue, which was her greatest fear. The last thing she wanted was to fly aimlessly through the elements on an endless search for something that might never be found, but she understood the stakes. She was acutely aware of her responsibilities.

The thought turned her bread to ash in her mouth, and fear coiled tighter with every imagined betrayal.

"I've packed your bags, Your Majesty," Kassandra said, her lips curving into a smile. "I've included some ginger root and other herbs for your nausea, as well as vitamins to keep you and the baby healthy on your journey. I truly hope you will be back home soon."

Aurelia nodded, glancing over Kassandra's shoulder as Cristos walked back into the room. "I hope so, too, Kassandra. Thank you for being so thoughtful. I'm sure you've packed everything I'll need."

With a dip of her chin and a small smile at Cristos, Kassandra slipped out of their chambers, leaving them alone. Aurelia pushed her plate of eggs and toast away, offering the remnants to her husband, who leaned over to kiss her.

"Exie and Septima are already heading down to the courtyard, along with Bremusa and the healer," he said, lowering himself into the chair beside her and taking a bite of her food. "Otera is sending a raven to the coast ahead of us to prepare a ship for our voyage to the west. We could fly over the Irriboia Sea, but storms are common, and we don't want to be caught over water during a storm."

A shiver ran down Aurelia's spine, a reminder of the significant risks they were taking. "I wouldn't want to be caught in a storm on a ship either," she replied.

Reaching out, Cristos wrapped his hand around hers, lifting it to kiss her knuckles. "We will have scouts with us who will fly ahead to keep an eye on the weather. If something is ahead, we'll do our best to navigate around it. I won't let anything happen to you, your sister, or Exie, and I won't let anything happen to our child. This, I can promise you."

Aurelia knew he meant what he said, and she trusted Cristos with her life, but they'd been through so much in such a short time, so although she trusted him, it was fate she did not trust. She didn't say that aloud. Instead, she leaned forward, sliding her hand around to cup the back of his head, the silky strands of his black hair threading through her fingers. "Do you think anyone would miss us if we took a little longer to get downstairs? I mean... It'll be a while before we find time alone together again, right?"

The curl of Cristos' lips against hers sent a shiver through Aurelia's body for a whole different reason than fear, temporarily sending their obligations to the back of her mind.

Sliding his arm around her back and another beneath her knees, Cristos lifted her from the chair, carrying her across the room to their bed, his lips never leaving hers as he walked. They didn't have a lot of time, but he was unhurried in the way he unlaced her tunic and slipped it down her shoulders, kissing her across her collarbone.

"We'll always find time to be alone, my queen, no matter where we are."

Pulling away from his lips, Aurelia grinned as she scooted back on the bed, wiggling free of her trousers and kicking them onto the floor. He did the same. "Even when we're in the air, my king? Will we find a way to be alone even then?"

The mischievous glint in his bright blue eyes always set her blood on fire. With the last of his clothing dropping to the ground, leaving his gorgeous, muscled body on full display beside the bed, he climbed over her, settling between her thighs. He dragged his length against her center, where she was already drenched for him. "I'll perch in a tree with you somewhere if I have to, but I'll get you alone somehow."

Before Aurelia could say anything more about his plans to make love to her in a tree, he thrust himself inside her, forcing a gasping breath from her lungs. Her fingernails dug into his shoulders below his outstretched wings, grasping for purchase as he hooked her leg around his hip, pressing in deeper. Sex between them had always been intense, a genuine bond between mates, but it had only grown more intense since they'd married, and even more so since she'd begun to transform to full-fae, since being mates had become part of her being as much as it was of his.

"You know I can't go too long without being inside you, my love," he whispered against her ear before kissing his way from her neck back to her lips, caressing her tongue with his. Inside her core, her climax built, the coil tightening with every roll of his hips against hers, his cock hitting that sensitive spot inside her that always drove her wild.

"I don't want to go without being with you either."

Their lips fused once more as his touch sent a ripple of heat down her spine. He knew how to make her feel alive in a way that no one else ever had. She loved Cristos with all her heart. They were a family, and they were continuing to build one together.

Cristos' hand skimmed along her back, kneading her skin in a way that made her shiver as his hips drove into her. He knew her body too well, knew how to wind her tight until every nerve strained for release, holding her on the brink until she was desperate for more.

When he finally gave it to her, Aurelia toppled over the edge with a cry against his mouth. The chamber, the world beyond their bed, ceased to exist—there was only the heat of his body, the thunder of his heart, and the relentless drive of his hips as he followed her into ecstasy. His kiss swallowed her moans, his muscles tightening as his own release surged through him, their pleasure crashing together until she was trembling beneath him.

With a final thrust, he let out a guttural groan, his release warming her insides as their breaths mingled between them. For a moment, all they could do was rest in bed together in each other's arms, hoping it was a moment they would be able to return to again soon.

The morning sun had just risen above the horizon when Aurelia and Cristos stepped out of Kano's enclosure and into the courtyard, leaving the relative safety of the palace behind. Aurelia gazed out over the Elder Sea, where the arched portal once stood—a haunting reminder of the father and brother she had just left behind. When she and Septima had agreed to give up their lives as humans and never look back, she had never thought of it as a decision that she couldn't one day reverse. She had never imagined that she would lose the possibility of returning to the human realm to see her family. But now...

Turning her head away from the sparkling water, Aurelia reached for Cristos' hand, interlacing her fingers with his as they walked toward Septima and the others, who were lingering near the barracks. She forced a smile when her sister glanced her way, despite the turmoil churning inside her.

With her sword strapped to her back, Septima stepped forward, her long ebony hair braided in her signature style, and pulled Aurelia into a hug. "How are you feeling this morning, Lia? Sick again?"

Aurelia shook her head, releasing Cristos' hand so he could continue toward the rest of their group and plot their course. There was so much to plan. "We were just trying to steal a few more moments alone before we can't for a while. None of us knows what we're heading into."

Septima's features softened as she rested her hand on Aurelia's forearm. "We'll find it, sissy. We have to. And when we do, we'll bring Amadeus—and maybe even Father—back to Ekotoria with us."

A snicker escaped Aurelia. "Could you imagine our father ever leaving Vaekros for any reason?"

Septima's smile faltered slightly as she pulled Aurelia closer, tucking her against her chest. "Maybe his priorities have changed since losing us."

There was no need to say that both of them hoped that was the case. They wished with all their hearts to reunite their family and get back the father they had once known before the loss of their mother had changed him and hardened his heart. But they both knew it was a fantasy. No matter how badly they wanted their father back, that man had died with the love of his life.

"Are you two ready?" Exie asked, moving to stand beside Septima, who reached forward to take the large pack from Exie's hands. Since Exie would have to shift into a phoenix, Septima would need to hook the bags onto the saddle. Several yards away, Cristos stood speaking to Kason and Holera, who were preparing to leave for their own mission to the southern part of the continent—back to Diapolis. Aurelia hoped that King Ailani had not betrayed them by taking the Shadow Glass; if he had, they would be walking into a trap. All they could do was have faith in Kason, Holera, and the shaky alliance with the isolationist king.

Forcing her eyes away from her husband, Aurelia turned back to look at Exie, who was still waiting for her answer, and nodded. "Do we know how long it will take to get to the coast?"

Exie glanced toward the west, as if she could see the other side of the continent beyond the tree canopy of the Spectre Forest. "If the weather holds, probably no longer than two days. If it doesn't... Let's just hope we can find a tavern along the coast with an inn."

The air grew thick with expectancy as they stepped out into the open courtyard of Flamecliff. A tapestry of faces lined the ramparts and courtyards, subjects and allies whose hopes clung to the bravery of those who dared to venture beyond the safety of stone walls.

"May the winds be a gentle caress at your backs," a veteran warrior called out, her voice carrying the weight of experience and unspoken fears.

"And the stars guide you through the darkest nights," a young acolyte added, her eyes bright with unshed tears.

A swell of emotion filled Aurelia's chest as she looked upon her people, their faces etched with a mix of admiration and anxiety. Their hope clung to her like a mantle—heavy yet fragile—and she knew that one misstep could shatter it. She raised a hand, not just in farewell, but as a silent vow that she would return, bringing with her the light of balance.

"Keep the hearths burning," she called back, her voice steady even as her heart raced against her ribs. "We shall return with the dawn."

The promise felt like iron on her tongue, a mix of vow and prayer.

Chapter Eight

Kason

Leaving Flamecliff toward Diapolis was a journey Kason and his mate had taken many times before, but this time felt different. The sky seemed wider than ever, yet each wingbeat carried the weight of suspicion and the unsettling thought of betrayal. They were uncertain about what awaited them. While they believed King Ailani had been their ally in the war against Joneira and Warbotach, they questioned whether he might use this opportunity to seize the Shadow Glass and betray them. The possibility that he was leading his mate into a trap tightened Kason's chest as he climbed onto her magnificent phoenix form. They launched into the air from the courtyard of the Aegrician palace. Every instinct urged him to turn back, yet duty bound him as if he were in chains. He was aware that they had obligations to their kingdom, so despite the risks, they had no choice but to fly south.

Settling on Holera's back, Kason rubbed her silky silver feathers, a gesture he always made when riding her. He watched the sparkling water below them. Even after so many years together, he would have preferred for her to ride on his back, but since she was the only one capable of becoming a phoenix, the only time she rode him was in their private moments. Just the thought of it sent blood rushing to his cock, making him

wish they could stop and camp for a few hours, just so she could indulge him.

"We can camp in the same place we stopped last time, my fierce warrior—if you would like," Holera said, lifting her head and opening her beak, her chest rumbling with agreement. Chuckling, he shifted his weight, ensuring their bags and weapons were secure on the saddle before massaging her neck again. It was a long flight, but that didn't mean he couldn't make it enjoyable for her by talking and touching her. Touching her was his favorite thing in the world, whether she had beautiful skin or silky feathers. As long as it was her, he would shower her with affection no matter the form she took.

Storm clouds gathered over the sea in the distance as the sun began its descent toward the horizon. However, it held off just long enough for Kason and Holera to reach the edge of Spectre Forest. Each flash of distant lightning seemed to serve as a warning from the gods that no journey could remain unchallenged.

Finding a clearing safe enough to set up camp, Holera landed, and Kason quickly dismounted, grabbing their supplies so she could shift back into her fae form. They barely had time to establish wards around their campsite, create a fire, and set up their tent before the rain began to fall. A canopy stretched from the front of their tent to a small grouping of trees a few feet away, allowing them to stay dry while they sat by the fire and ate a simple dinner of meat and fruit.

"After this trip south," Holera began, leaning her head on Kason's shoulder as he wrapped his arm around her smaller frame and pulled her closer, "I hope we can return to our cottage and maybe visit my mother."

Kason nodded, kissing the top of her head. "I would like that, as would she." He exhaled slowly, hesitating to choose his next words. He wondered if it was the wrong moment to speak, but he dared to express his thoughts anyway. "Maybe we can stay home for a while... start a family."

The words felt fragile in his mouth, like spun glass— a dream so delicate it might shatter under the weight of war. Silence stretched between them, the hooting of an owl in the distance making Kason think that perhaps mentioning children had been a mistake. Just as his mind began to chastise him for pressuring her, Holera lifted her face, her violet eyes meeting his. What he saw within them told him she was not opposed to the idea at all. "You would be an amazing father."

Unable to contain himself, Kason leaned over and kissed her. "And you would make a fierce, stunning, wonderful mother." He raised an eyebrow, sliding his hand up Holera's thigh, skimming over the heated fabric between her legs, and resting on the lower part of her flat stomach. "And just the thought of seeing you pregnant with my child has me ready to burst through my trousers. So how about we go to bed?"

Although fatigue weighed down Holera's features, the corners of her lips curled into a grin. "I suppose we should practice for when that time comes."

Chuckling, Kason stood and reached down to help her to her feet. "We can practice as often as you would like to, my mate."

With the pot of water they'd heated over the fire in hand, Kason followed his sleepy mate into their tent, sealing the entrance behind them.

"Would you like a bath, my flame? We don't have a tub, but we've got hot water and my hands. There's probably a little soap in my satchel."

A cascade of Holera's silky platinum hair slid over her shoulder as she turned her head to look at him, the side of her mouth tipping up as her trousers dropped to the floor, pooling at her feet.

"Are you offering to bathe me, my love?" Twisting around to face him, her slender fingers threaded into the laces of her tunic, Kason's eyes tracking the movement as she pulled them loose achingly slowly. Even after decades together, she was the most exquisite creature he'd ever seen. The years had not dulled her fire, though the exhaustion etched into her eyes reminded him how fiercely she had carried their people through endless battles. He craved her on a carnal level that only mates could understand. It was a hunger that could never be sated, and he didn't want it to. Every second he got to spend with her made him the happiest male in the world.

Kason nodded, dragging his tongue across his lips. "It would be my pleasure."

Holera took a step forward, her tunic slipping down her shoulders, her pink nipples pebbled against the chill.

"You can't bathe me if you're just going to stand there with the pot of water in your hands, my love."

His cock throbbing painfully against his zipper, Kason set the pot down beside their bedding and then reached for her, wrapping his lips around her nipple.

Holera's back arched as he sucked on the tender flesh, her fingers threading into his long hair and pulling out the cord tying it back. The bucket of water beside his feet was forgotten as he wrapped his arm beneath her legs and scooped her up, carrying her to the bedroll. "I don't mind it if you're a little bit dirty, my warrior."

"This I kn—ow—" Words turning into a moan, Holera's head fell back as Kason's hand trailed up her thigh, leaving a trickle of warm water across her skin. His hands caressed her leg from her hip to her toes, caressing her skin with just enough warm water to soothe and clean her.

The fire outside their tent still flickered, illuminating the side of her stunning face as her mouth fell open, a gasp escaping on a breath when his tongue slid between her folds to taste her. "You taste delicious to me, my mate."

Everything about her was perfection. No matter where they were—what they'd gone through together—his fierce warrior was perfection. How her body welcomed him inside, warm and wet, how her sharp nails scraped along his back until he growled her name against her lips. There was no female in their world, or in any, who could have set his world on fire like she did.

When they fell asleep that night, with the crackle of the fire and the distant sounds of the forest to lull them to sleep, all Kason could think of was returning home to a peaceful kingdom with his mate, so he could take her back to their cottage and fill her with his child. In that vision of hearth and home, he saw not just survival, but the promise of a future worth every wound he carried.

Chapter Nine

Aurelia

The first leg of their trip toward the western coast of Ekotoria had been relatively uneventful, giving Aurelia and Cristos plenty of time to talk as he held her against his chest—the same way he'd held her whenever they traveled together. Exie and Septima flew alongside them, Exie in her phoenix form and Septima astride her back. There were several other people in their party, including Bremusa, who flew as a brilliant golden phoenix, competing with the rays of the sun at high noon. The space beneath Aurelia's shoulder blades tingled with the need to release her wings and fly, but having only just received them, she was not confident in her ability to fly safely. There was so much she needed to learn about the changes to her body first. Plus, she loved being in her mate's arms—strong and incredibly warm—as he spoke just inside her ear. "You've gone quiet, my wife. What's going on in that pretty head of yours?"

Cristos nuzzled into her neck, his lips pressing against her skin as his powerful wings flew them over Spectre Forest. Shivers raced down Aurelia's spine, her body coming alive under his affections even as her mind had indeed drifted. "I was just thinking about my mother... How frightening it must have been to be pregnant while knowing people wanted to kill her, knowing they wanted to kill *me*."

As though he wasn't holding her tightly enough, Cristos pulled her closer, his muscles tightening. "Is that when your parents moved to the city—in hopes that being within the kingdom's walls would keep her protected?"

Aurelia nodded. "My parents moved back to the mainland of Vaekros when my mother was pregnant with Amadeus, although I know she preferred to remain in Breqan. We were never told about my mother's fae heritage, so I never knew about her thoughts or fears growing up, but looking back..."

For a moment, she fell silent, pain making the backs of her eyes burn. In her periphery, she glanced at her sister, Septima's long braids whipping in the wind as she leaned over and held onto the reins of Exie's saddle. As though she could feel her sister's stare, Septima turned her deep brown eyes to Aurelia's, a question in them. Her lips mouthed the words: "Are you okay?"

Even though Aurelia knew her eyes were glassy, she nodded and smiled. When they stopped for the night, they could talk, and judging by the position of the sun, it wouldn't be long before they did so.

"You never knew your lives were in danger?"

So caught up in her own head, Cristos' question caught Aurelia by surprise. She shook her head, leaning into his warmth. The lower the sun sunk toward the horizon, the cooler the temperature became. "I never knew any of it. As far as I knew, we were ordinary humans. The most danger we were ever in was the risk of war when our kingdom became too power-hungry. When my mother got sick... When they told us—"

Her throat constricted with the words, knowing they had always been a lie but remembering how it felt to be so young and know her mother was dying on the other side of the wooden door and to be not allowed to go inside and save her, to be unable to turn the knob and tell her mother goodbye and that she loved her. No matter how much time had passed, the pain of losing her mother never eased. She only wished she had a painting of her mother's face, but Otera looked so much like her. Even her own face, her red hair and blue eyes were her mother's, but it wasn't the same. There had been something so special about Messalina Lumino, the kindness in her heart and the beauty in her smile, that could never be replaced.

Shaking her head, she tried to force the vision from her mind. "Even when they told us my mother was sick, they kept us away. We weren't allowed to go near her at risk of catching her illness—weren't allowed to say goodbye. Now I know it was because she wasn't sick at all. It was all a lie."

As the sun set below the horizon and stars lit up the moonless sky, Aurelia and the rest of their group descended into Spectre Forest to find a place to camp for the night. After such a long day, Aurelia would have loved to spend the night in a tavern where she could sleep on a real mattress, but there were no cities in the center of the continent, so it wasn't an option. When they reached the coast, she hoped that would change.

Setting down in a clearing near a small stream, Bremusa immediately began erecting wards around their perimeter to protect them from any passersby, while a few of the others gathered wood for a fire. As Exie and Cristos erected tents, Aurelia joined her sister near the stream, filling pots with water to cook a stew with the dried meats and vegetables they'd packed for their journey. Everyone had a part to play, a role to keep things running smoothly and safely. As queen, some would have expected Aurelia to retire to her tent and prop her feet up, especially with her being pregnant, but that wasn't who she was, and she had no intention of hiding away while everyone else did the work. So, while she couldn't do the most labor-intensive jobs at their camp, she could cook, so that was what she chose to do.

"What was wrong earlier?" Septima asked, hanging the pot over the already blazing fire, her expression not hiding her concern. "It was clear across your face, even though I know you tried to hide it behind a smile."

With the last of the meat sinking into the stew broth, Aurelia fell back on her heels, warming her hands by the fire.

"Do you ever think we're just chasing ghosts?"

For the next several minutes, as they watched the food boil over an open flame, Septima and Aurelia shared their thoughts about the mission they were on. They'd left the capital so quickly—the embers from battle barely turned into ash in the wind—so there had barely been time to discuss the journey they were going on and what they would do if they found nothing. The last thing Aurelia wanted was to be a pessimist, but she was queen of a kingdom that she'd only just laid her eyes on, and was expected to somehow merge the northern half of the continent based on a prophecy spoken before she had even been born.

With the king of Norithae already her husband, part of her work was already done for her, but they had cities to rebuild and people to rally. Although Cristos had been raised in the monarchy, neither of them had ever ruled before. They had so much to do and so much to lead Luckily they had one valuable resource willing to be there for them every step of the way: *Otera*. The list of what they had to do continued to get longer with every day that passed, but with Otera as their mentor, Aurelia only hoped they didn't let their people down.

While the small group ate around the fire, they discussed the next leg of their journey, which would take them to the western coast of Ekotoria—a place Aurelia had yet to see. If it were for any other reason, she would have been excited to explore her world. Still, it sounded, at least from the plans their group was making, as though they would be exploring parts of their world that even Cristos had yet to see. The idea was exciting, but they didn't know what they might encounter, and that made it scary as well.

Chapter Ten

Taryn

A crimson sun rose over the jagged mountains, casting a warm glow on Taryn's face as she lay in bed. The warmth seemed to mock her, gilding a face that felt as though it had been carved from sorrow. She blinked away the remnants of sleep and stretched, her heart heavy with the loss of her mate and the guilt of finding solace in Lars' embrace. Taryn knew she couldn't wallow in self-pity forever; there was work to be done.

Blowing out a breath, she swung her legs out of bed and quickly dressed in a tunic and trousers. As soon as she stepped out of her tent and walked through the camp, joining the throng of workers, she spotted Otera and Blaedia standing amidst the chaos. The former queen and her mate surveyed the damage. They directed the rebuilding efforts after the devastation caused not only by the war but also by the destruction of the portal.

"Good morning, Taryn," Otera said, her voice gentle as the morning breeze.

"Morning," Taryn replied, attempting a smile that didn't quite reach her eyes. "What can I do to help?"

"Help us tend to the injured warriors," Blaedia suggested, gesturing to a makeshift infirmary nearby. "They need our strength now more than ever."

Nodding, Taryn followed them toward the rows of wounded males and females. As they worked together, cleaning wounds and applying healing poultices, Taryn felt a gnawing ache in the pit of her stomach. She looked around, taking in the pain etched on the faces of those who had survived while others perished. Her own life had been spared when she'd been brought back from the brink of death, but so many others hadn't been so fortunate. Each breath she drew felt stolen, borrowed from the lungs of those who no longer had a chance.

"Otera," Taryn murmured, swallowing hard as she glanced at her friend. "How do you deal with it? The guilt, I mean."

"Ah." With a sigh, Otera paused her work to meet Taryn's gaze. "There's no easy answer, my friend. We all carry our burdens, but we must also remember that our lives have been given back to us for a reason."

"Exactly," Blaedia chimed in, her voice firm yet kind. "We are phoenix warriors, Taryn. We rise from the ashes of defeat and continue to fight for those who can't."

But rising again only deepened the fissures inside her, for some wounds could not be cauterized by flame.

Taking a deep breath, Taryn allowed their words to wash over her like a soothing balm. Her survivor's guilt still weighed on her heart, and the loss of her mate made her feel as though her heart was torn in two and bleeding. Yet, she knew that wallowing in her pain would do no good. Instead, she needed to channel her energy into helping rebuild Flamecliff and healing those who needed her.

"Thank you," she whispered, her eyes glistening with unshed tears. "I'll try my best to make every moment count."

"Always, Taryn." Otera smiled, placing a reassuring hand on her shoulder. "Together, we will rise again."

The night descended upon Flamecliff like a velvet shroud, draping the realm in hues of deep purples and somber blues. Taryn's heart, a tempest of sorrow and remorse, sought shelter from its relentless storm. The labor of the day had dulled the edge of her anguish, but now, as the night sky whispered secrets to the stars, her soul yearned for solace that stone and mortar could not provide.

The waters of the Elder Sea sparkled beneath the moon and stars as Taryn's phoenix form perched high on the Aegrician cliffs, watching schools of fish swim happily below the surface, oblivious to the predator lurking nearby. Fortunately for them, she wasn't hungry. Despite not having eaten in days, she had no appetite. Blaedia would say she was torturing herself, punishing herself for what had happened to her mate, but it didn't matter to her.

While she had been with another male the night before they went into battle, her mate had been struck down in a rebel uprising in the city streets outside the palace. As she spent that night with another male, the one she was never meant to be with, her mate was taking his last breath. She hated herself for it. If she was punishing herself by not eating, then so be it; she deserved it, at least in her own mind. The destruction of the portal had brought her back from the ashes, forcing life back into her when so many others had not been so lucky. Out of all the people who had died in that war, she did not feel deserving of a second life.

Letting out a call of mourning that echoed across the silent sea, the cry broke from her chest like a rift in stone—unyielding and uncontainable, scattering into the night as though the stars themselves might carry it. She launched herself off the cliff, soaring over the sea toward the Norithaean camp they had set up just outside the city, using the talisman around her neck to pass through their wards. Once inside the camp, which resembled their own, she didn't mingle; instead, she headed straight for the row of tents lining the back of the camp, slipping through the tent flap.

"Taryn," Lars murmured, rising from his makeshift bed to embrace her. His strong arms enfolded her like a protective cocoon, shielding her from the harsh realities outside. "I've been really worried about you."

Ever since that night they had spent together in the mountain valley, she had been using him as a distraction—or at least that's what she had told herself. The truth was, Lars was incredibly handsome, with long chestnut hair, golden eyes, and majestic leathery wings. Yet every day, she spiraled deeper into self-loathing. Once more, she found herself within the canvas confines of Lars' tent, trembling hands reaching for the male whose very touch ignited a firestorm of forbidden pleasure. She craved to feel something—anything—aside from her guilt and pain. Yet every kiss was lined with ash, every caress a reminder that her heart had become both a tomb and a battlefield. Lars never failed to evoke feelings within her.

"Have you?" Suppressed emotion trembled in her voice as she buried her face in the crook of his neck, inhaling his scent—earth and fire mingling with the faintest hint of sea spray.

"Of course," he replied, his breath warm against her ear. When he pulled back slightly, his golden eyes searched her face as if attempting to read her thoughts. "You've been carrying so much weight on your shoulders lately."

She nodded, unable to deny the truth in his words as she un-buttoned her cloak, hanging it on an empty chair. "It's too quiet everywhere but inside my head. I can't stop thinking about what we all lost—about those who deserved so much better."

Tucking a lock of her dark hair behind her ear, Lars dipped his chin, understanding without needing more explanation from her. He hadn't yet found his mate, and she didn't feel deserving of ever having one, so they found something in each other. Cassius had only been dead for a few days, but she'd spent every night since in Lars' bed—every night since she'd come back from across the veil, or wherever she'd gone when she'd taken a sword to her heart.

Threading his fingers into her hair, he tipped her head back, forcing her to look at him. He knew she didn't want to meet his eyes, but he wasn't giving her the option. "Let me help you forget, even if it's just for a little while?"

Everything inside of her said no, torn between her loyalty to her lost mate and her need for physical connection. But in the end, her desire for an escape won out, so she nodded, rising on the tips of her toes and pressing her lips to his. Lars was slow to respond, sending her already broken heart plummeting into her stomach, but as though he could sense it, he wrapped his arms around her, deepening the kiss.

Taryn met his tongue stroke for stroke, needing to forget the loss she'd suffered and how the dark pit inside of her seemed to grow and fester with each breath. Slipping her hands between their bodies, she reached for the clasp on his trousers, never leaving their kiss as she released his hardness from its confines. To her relief, he didn't stop her, and he wasn't gentle with her. Instead, he unbuckled her trousers, shoving them down her thighs while his mouth kissed and sucked hers, the touch desperate.

"Turn around," he said, his deep voice raspy with lust. "Hold on to the table. I want to see your pretty cunt in the air."

She didn't hesitate to obey, to turn around and brace herself against the table as his powerful thrusts forced so much pleasure into her body that the hurt had no choice but to hide away in the shadows for a while. A fierce blaze consumed them, their bodies entwined in desperate abandon. As she pulled in shaky breaths, Taryn held onto the table with Lars' muscular form draped over her, his seed trailing down her thigh. For a moment, she tried not to think, allowing her eyes to close and the afterglow of her orgasm to flow through her body, to bring in the light, but there were some places it couldn't go.

"Thank you." Although she hadn't intended the words and wasn't sure what she'd meant by them, they'd found their way through her lips, and she hadn't missed the way Lars' body flinched.

"Thank me, for what?" Straightening, he backed up a few steps, grabbing a rag to wipe them clean. The absence of him inside of her was agony, and all she wanted, at that moment, was for him to slide back inside her, but the confusion on his face told her the moment had shifted. "This isn't a business transaction, Taryn, and I'm not doing it just to do you a favor. You don't have to thank me."

His response to her gratitude was jarring, raising an alarm inside her chest. "I wasn't trying to upset you, Lars. It's just that..." Guilt and grief, heavy and throbbing, took root in her chest, forcing the air from her lungs.

Reaching for her tunic, she pulled it over her head quickly before tugging her trousers up her legs, barely turning to look at him as she headed toward the tent flap. Before she stepped out into the chilly night air, with her hand wrapped around the tent flap, she spoke without looking back. "I'm just really sorry, Lars. I'm sorry for all of it. I'm sorry for using you, so I wouldn't have to dwell in my grief, so I wouldn't have to accept my role in everything my people have lost. I'm just...sorry."

Clad in nothing but regret, Taryn slipped out of Lars's tent, feeling the cool air caress her skin as she shifted into her phoenix form. Her fiery wings unfurled like banners of defiance against the starry sky. Her skin still burned from his touch, but it was a fire that offered no warmth—only a reminder that desire could not silence grief. Her heart raced with echoes of their passionate encounter. Still, she needed to clear her mind and find some semblance of balance amidst the turmoil threatening to engulf her.

As she soared above Flamecliff, the sea stretched out below her like a vast, unending expanse of midnight silk. Her keen senses detected a strange undercurrent—an unsettling rumbling that seemed to resonate from the very heart of the sea itself.

Suddenly, the ground beneath her shook violently, as if the world itself were convulsing in pain. The tremors felt personal, as though the realm mirrored the fracture within her. The powerful earthquake sent shockwaves through the land, causing buildings to tremble and people to cry out in fear and confusion.

Landing near the palace, Taryn watched from the parapet as the sea roiled and churned before her eyes, transforming into a monstrous wave that defied nature itself. It towered over the harbor of Flamecliff, casting a massive shadow that stretched far across the land. In an instant, the tidal wave crashed down with an earth-shattering roar, obliterating everything in its path.

CHAPTER ELEVEN

AURELIA

As Aurelia slept beside Cristos in their tent in Spectre Forest, time's relentless march slowed, momentarily retracing its steps under the influence of a memory. It broke through her dreams, which were little more than fantasies. Much like the forest surrounding her, she found herself in the lush embrace of another place—the Howling Forest. The dream unfolded with a clarity so sharp it stung, as if memory itself had been lying in wait. Sunlight played hide and seek among the leaves, dappling the forest floor with patches of warmth. In this dream, the air whispered secrets that only the trees could understand, and the only struggle was between one's imperfections and the pursuit of mastery.

"Focus, little bird," said the mellifluous voice of her mother, its tone resonating with an ancient wisdom that filled Aurelia with boundless respect and affection. "Let your breath guide the arrow—let your spirit calm the storm within you."

Her mother's presence was a soothing balm, her guidance the compass by which Aurelia navigated her young life. With wide eyes, filled with the innocence of youth and the determination to make her mother proud, she drew the bowstring with hesitant strength.

"See how the bow becomes an extension of your being," Messalina continued, gently correcting Aurelia's stance. "You are not separate from it, nor is it from you. Together, you create harmony in tension, potential waiting to be released."

"Like the wind cradles the hawk aloft?" Even at her young age, the metaphor flowed from her lips with newfound understanding.

With a brilliant smile that radiated pure love, Messalina nodded. "That's right, my sweet. Now, release."

Messalina's words glowed in Aurelia's chest, imprinting a lesson that would endure even beyond her mother's breath.

Aurelia's eyes snapped open as the earth subtly shuddered beneath her, a sinister whisper against the forest floor underneath their tent. Her heart quickened, an erratic drumbeat echoing the unease that slithered through her veins. It felt as if the land itself breathed uneasily beneath them, restless in its grief. Beside her, Cristos shot up on the bedroll, reaching for her to ensure she was okay.

Without taking a moment to process the disruption in their slumber, they dressed quickly. By the time they stepped outside the tent, they found the others already gathered, their faces etched with concern in the dawn's half-light filtering through the tree canopy. In the center stood Bremusa, her silver eyes cradling the secrets of the cosmos within their depths.

"The very sinews of Ekotoria tremble with longing for what has been stolen from its grasp—the portal. Its absence is a gaping wound in the fabric of our realm," she declared.

Nausea twisted in Aurelia's stomach at the elemental's words, sending bile rising in her throat. "Could it be creating such a drastic effect on the land already?" she asked.

Bremusa nodded, gazing up at the sky while her obsidian hair slid over her shoulder. "Time weaves an intricate and obscure tapestry. Yet, each thread quivers with purpose. These circumstances are unprecedented, but if my senses are correct, the balance of our continent teeters on the edge of ruin without the portal's power to anchor it."

Her words fell like stones into Aurelia's gut, each one a reminder that destiny has no patience for the unprepared.

With the earth trembling beneath them, the small band of warriors, including Aurelia, sprang into action. Tents were dismantled, and bedrolls were tightly bound, every item of their hasty encampment quickly swallowed by packs as if it had never existed.

As they returned to the clearing with their supplies packed, Aurelia secured her bow and quiver to her shoulder and took her husband's hand.

"Ready, my love?" he asked, unfurling his mighty wings, a dark canvas against the lightening sky.

The tremors had stopped. There had only been one, but Aurelia still scanned the forest, wondering how far the epicenter had been and hoping it wasn't in Aegricia.

As the rest of their group began to launch into the air, heading toward the coast, Aurelia allowed herself to be lifted into Cristos' embrace. Beside them, Septima stood next to Exie as her mate shifted—Exie's golden hair catching the newborn sun's rays, igniting like the flames from which they were born. With a cry that split the dawn's stillness, Exie leaped skyward, her colorful wings lifting them above the forest in moments.

Once Septima and Exie disappeared from view, Cristos' wings made a powerful downbeat, and they ascended, soaring above the treetops, leaving only the ghost of their presence lingering in the air.

The western coast of Ekotoria unveiled itself like a forgotten verse from an ancient tome, its rugged cliffs and sapphire waters taking Aurelia's breath away. Yet, the beauty could not soften the edge of her unease; even the waves seemed to whisper warnings in their endless rhythm. They had been flying for most of the day, and while the flight had been quiet, peaceful even, they were all exhausted when the sea came into view. Aurelia's gaze swept across the quaint hamlet as they descended, the brine of the sea infiltrating her senses and reminding her of home.

"Looks like a good place to lay low for the night," Cristos murmured into Aurelia's ear, the warmth of his breath sending shivers down her spine.

Leaning into his muscular frame, Aurelia nodded. "It'll be nice to get a bath and sleep in a real bed."

Cristos chuckled, angling his wings to land. "That it will, and maybe there will be whispers of what we're searching for—something that can lead us in the right direction."

Aurelia shrugged and glanced at her sister, who was already unsheathing her sword. She surveyed the haphazard collection of wooden buildings that made up the town. It looked humble enough, but in the land of the fae, appearances could be deceiving. "As long as they're friendly."

As soon as his boots touched the ground, Cristos set Aurelia down beside him but reached for her hand. "Stay close. We don't know what we'll find here."

The group wove through the narrow streets, taking in the sights and sounds of the bustling harbor town. Locals exchanged gossip as they tended to their chores or bartered over goods, seemingly unaware of the king and queen's presence among them, which was exactly how Aurelia wanted it. She pulled her hood over her head to draw less attention to herself. The locals may not have known her, but they certainly recognized her aunt, who looked very much like her.

"Over there." Exie pointed to a worn-looking tavern with a crooked sign that read "The Salty Serpent." "It may not be the finest establishment, but it should suffice for our needs."

Inside, the air was thick with the smell of ale and roasting meat. The patrons eyed the newcomers warily but didn't let their curiosity interrupt their conversations. Exie and Septima approached the barkeep, a grizzled man with a patch over one eye, and inquired about renting a room. Aurelia and Cristos stood off to the side, studying the room.

"Only got three left," he grunted, handing her three tarnished keys. "Upstairs, second door on the right. Payment will be due in the morning."

"Thank you," Septima replied, slipping a few coins onto the counter. "We'll be sure to settle our debt before we leave."

"See that you do," the barkeep said, eyeing the coins with an expression Aurelia couldn't quite place.

As her companions settled around a large table near the back of the room, Aurelia couldn't shake the nagging feeling that they were being watched. She glanced around the dimly lit tavern, trying to discern any signs of danger or deceit. Every shadow seemed to lean closer, and every whisper was laced with secrets meant to pierce.

"Keep your ears open," Cristos whispered across the table. "We need to learn what we can about this place, its people, and any information regarding the missing portal or the rebel groups operating nearby."

"Of course," Exie replied, reaching for a tankard of ale and taking a slow sip. "Let's see what we can overhear."

For the next few hours, while they ate their dinner—everyone but Aurelia enjoying a pint of ale—the group listened intently to the other patrons. Their eyes darted between various tables as they tried to glean helpful information from the snippets of conversation drifting through the air. But by the time Aurelia was yawning and the group was ready for bed, they were no wiser than when they had entered.

Aurelia's reflection shimmered in the moonlit window, her gaze drawn to the silver curve of the crescent moon against the distant horizon. Beside her, Cristos' muscular frame filled

the doorway, his leathery wings folded tightly against his back as he stepped into their rented room at the tavern.

"Did you find anything?" she asked, her voice soft and tentative.

Closing the door behind him, he crossed the room toward her. "Nothing concrete, but we won't give up, my love. We will find the portal, I promise."

As he reached her side, Aurelia leaned into him, seeking solace in the warmth of his embrace. The weight of their quest bore down on her, but in Cristos' arms, she found a reprieve from her worries. She turned to face him, locking her eyes with his, filled with love and understanding.

"Thank you," she whispered, lifting her hands to cup his face. "It can be so overwhelming at times."

Leaning forward, he pressed a gentle kiss to her forehead. "Let me help shoulder that burden, my queen. Together, we can face anything."

With no more words to express her doubts, their lips met in a passionate embrace, hearts pounding in unison as they lost themselves in one another. In that moment, their connection transcended words, the depth of their love shining like a beacon in the darkness that surrounded them.

Wrapping his arms around her, Cristos lifted Aurelia and carried her to the bed, laying her down on the blankets and crawling on top of her.

"Remember," he breathed into her ear, his voice deep and husky, "we are bound by more than love. We are bound by fate, and destiny has chosen us to restore balance to Aegricia."

Lowering his lips to hers once more, Cristos kissed her thoroughly, slowly, and deeply. Their bodies entwined, every touch conveying the intensity of their love and desire for one another.

In the midst of their intimate moment, a sudden explosion shook the tavern's foundations, and the sound of screams and clashing weapons filled the air. Aurelia and Cristos sprang apart, their hearts pounding for an entirely different reason.

"An attack," Cristos growled, his eyes flashing with rage. "If the rebels recognized us, they'll try to assassinate us."

Pulling on her clothing without a second thought, Aurelia reached for her weapons, securing them in place. "Quickly, we must help the others."

The resounding clang of steel on steel echoed through the smoke-filled streets, its harsh staccato punctuated by cries of pain and fury from both friend and foe alike. Aurelia's heart pounded against her chest like a wild bird seeking escape, the heat of battle and her fierce love for her people fueling every move. She danced through the chaos, her bow singing death as it unleashed arrow after arrow into the bodies of the rebels in red robes—those who killed indiscriminately as they advanced down the streets.

"Stay together!" she shouted to her companions, her eyes scanning the scene. Cristos fought by her side, his sword flashing like lightning as he cut down anyone who dared approach them. The others had spread out, each engaging in their own skirmishes amidst the destruction.

"Quickly, to the harbor!" Bremusa urged, her silver eyes alight with the intensity of her elemental powers. "We must reach our ship before they overwhelm us!"

Aurelia nodded, and the group began to fight their way toward the harbor, their movements swift and purposeful. They encountered enemy after enemy; the rebels' crimson capes, like apparitions of blood, were everywhere they looked, but their determination never wavered. Septima and Exie moved in perfect harmony, their swords a blur of lethal precision. At the same time, Bremusa unleashed torrents of fire upon their foes.

"Almost there!" Aurelia called, her voice strained but hopeful as they neared the water's edge.

As the group approached the harbor, they were met with a horrifying sight: two of their warriors, Rockie and Nikoleta, lay sprawled upon the ground, bloodied and unconscious. Aurelia's heart clenched at the sight, but she knew they had no time to grieve or tend to their wounds. They needed to escape, and they needed to do it immediately.

"Help me with them!" Aurelia cried, her voice breaking as she struggled to lift Rockie's limp form. Cristos moved in to assist, his strong arms easily hoisting the warrior onto his shoulder, while Septima and Exie helped with Nikoleta.

"Leave us," a weak voice whispered, and Aurelia looked down in shock to see Rockie's eyes flutter open. "You must go. We will only slow you down."

Closing her eyes for only a moment, she shook her head. "Let's go!" she shouted, and the group made their final push to the ship, cutting down any adversaries that stood in their way. They scrambled aboard and set sail just as a fresh wave of enemies surged toward them. The wind caught their sails, carrying them away from the burning town of Shadewater and toward the uncertain future that awaited them in the Inferno Territories.

Behind them, smoke clawed at the heavens, a dark hand reaching to drag them back, but the sea pulled them forward into fate's uncharted waters.

Chapter Twelve

Kason

Emerging from the shadows, Kason and Holera entered Embershell, the capital city of Diapolis, through the massive city gates. Disguising themselves as weary travelers, Kason's piercing green eyes swept over the bustling urban district, the hood of his cloak pulled over his head to hide the intricate tattoos snaking up his neck. He and his mate had been to Embershell before, so remaining undercover would not be easy. Beside him, Holera's silver hair had been dyed black, allowing her to better blend into the shadows.

"Keep close, love," Kason murmured, his voice a low rumble only Holera could discern amid the cacophony of haggling merchants and boisterous street performers. His hand, discreet beneath his cloak, found hers, his thumb tracing the archer's calluses born from a thousand released arrows.

"If we're going to manage to not draw attention to ourselves," she said, glancing up at him with a smirk. "You'll have to manage not to get into any bar fights."

Kason chuckled, lifting her hand to kiss her knuckles. They were a formidable team, both in love and in battle, taking on everything together. "I'll do my best."

As they strolled through the lively streets of Embershell, they came upon a tavern named The Dragon's Roost. Its facade was a tapestry of timeworn stones, its sign creaking gently in the sea breeze, depicting a dragon curled around a chalice with scales glistening under the flicker of torchlight. As they stood outside, one of the winged beasts flew overhead, its roar echoing through the night.

Sliding his arm around Holera's back, Kason pulled the door open, ushering her inside.

Inside the raucous establishment, the scent of spiced meat mingled with the tang of sea salt from the nearby docks. Kason led the way to a table nestled in the seclusion of a shadowy nook.

"Perfect for an evening of espionage," he said, the hint of a smile playing on his lips. Once Holera slid into the booth, he slid in beside her, wrapping his arm around her waist and lifting his hand to the server. They'd been traveling for two days, so he was more than ready to get his mate into bed and start fresh in the morning. After he ordered two ales and a room for the night, Kason leaned back against the wall, stretching his long legs out beneath the table. Holera pulled her bow and quiver from her back, leaning it against the table within arm's reach—a habit born from necessity. Her gaze flitted across the room, sharp and observant, missing nothing. Laughter erupted from a group of sailors across the room, their tales of monstrous sea creatures louder than the rest.

Their ale arrived shortly thereafter, served by a grizzled bartender with a face weathered by years of hard living. Kason took a long sip, relishing the bitter taste as it slid down his throat. Beside him, Holera tore into her meal as though she hadn't eaten all day. When Kason gave it some thought, he realized they hadn't eaten much that day since they'd spent so many hours on horseback.

"Is it tasty, my fierce warrior? Or are you preparing to eat for two?" Even as he chuckled, she shot him a scowl—one that was meant to appear vicious—but it only made her look sexier.

Sliding his hand up her toned thigh, he leaned over to whisper in her ear. "I bet it's not as tasty as you are."

With the piece of fish still in her mouth as she tried to chew, she rolled her hips against his hand beneath the table, seemingly unworried if someone was watching them.

With the number of patrons in the tavern, listening in to any one conversation was nearly impossible. Holera's gaze flitted across the room, taking in the patrons who were as varied as the many realms they hailed from—merchants, sailors, adventurers, all with stories etched on their faces. For the first hour, they listened to the conversations going on around them, hoping to catch any whispers of intrigue or betrayal. But the talk was of mundane matters—local gossip, tales of adventure, the boasts of prowess in battle. Sipping on ale and dining on grilled fish and vegetables, Holera and Kason listened to mindless chatter and the tunes of a half-drunken bard. Kason's frustration grew with each passing minute, his patience wearing thin as the night went on.

Their mission weighed heavily on Kason's mind, a shadow that lurked in the corners of his thoughts, waiting to be brought into the light. They were there to uncover the truth, to discover if the King of Diapolis had betrayed them, and if he'd stolen the legendary Shadow Glass while everyone else had been too distracted by the war to notice. As they sat at the table in the back of the tavern, Kason couldn't shake the feeling of unease that gnawed at him. The war had left scars on all the kingdoms involved, wounds that still festered beneath the surface, and it was well-known that King Alani was an isolationist. If the Shadow Glass had fallen into the wrong hands, it could tip the delicate balance of power on Ekotoria, plunging the realm into chaos once more.

When the hourglass of patience had all but drained, a young barmaid with a coquettish smile stopped by their table, refilling their ale. "Anything else I can get you two lovebirds?" she purred, her eyes lingering on Kason's tattooed bicep.

Holera's violet eyes narrowed playfully, her possessive hand resting on Kason's. "We're fine for now, thank you," she said, the steel in her voice unmistakable. The barmaid retreated, casting a pouting glance over her shoulder.

"Jealous?" Kason teased, draping an arm around her shoulders.

Leaning into his side, she nibbled his earlobe. "Not if I can help it, but if she comes back—"

With a chuckle, he slid his hand up to cradle the back of her head, pulling her into a kiss. For a moment, as his tongue slipped inside to taste the female who was his in every way, the world around them disappeared, but like a spark igniting tinder, the atmosphere shifted. Two merchants entered the tavern, their voices low and conspiratorial as they took a seat nearby. Kason leaned forward, his senses alert as he strained to catch their conversation.

"They say the caves off the coast are filled with treasures beyond imagining," one of the merchants said, his voice a low murmur that still made it to Kason's ears. "Objects of magic, they say, more precious than the golden statues of Lyrandar."

"Aye, but they're guarded by powerful wards," the other replied, his tone cautious. "Only those with the right connections can gain access."

Kason exchanged a glance with Holera, a silent understanding passing between them.

"They speak of high-valued objects," Holera murmured, her voice barely audible above the din of the tavern. "If the king is hiding the Shadow Glass, it could be hidden in those caves."

"Another shipment is due to arrive in three days' time," one of the merchants said as he took a deep sip of his drink. "If we can secure it, we'll be set for life."

The mention of a shipment sent Kason's heart into a quickened beat. Three days' time... If the shipment contained the Shadow Glass, they had a deadline, a window of opportunity to uncover the truth before it slipped through their fingers.

The flickering glow of candlelight danced upon the walls of their modest room above the tavern, casting gentle shadows that lent an air of intimacy to the space. Holera stood by the window, her hair cascading down her back like a silken waterfall as she gazed out at the moonlit landscape. Kason watched her for a moment, admiring the serene beauty she exuded even in moments of quiet contemplation.

"Let me run you a bath, love" he said as he stepped up behind her and kissed her neck, breaking the silence that had enveloped them. Holera turned her face up to smile at him, her violet eyes reflecting how tired she was after such a long two days of travel.

"That sounds lovely, thank you."

When Kason was finished filling the copper tub with steaming water, Holera slipped out of her clothing in the bedchamber, hardening him with more desire than should have been physically possible, but he pushed it back. After spending the night before in a tent, he knew how badly she wanted a bath, and taking care of her needs was always his priority.

Once the tub was full, he gestured for her to step into the bath, his strong arms steadying her as she lowered herself into the inviting embrace of the water. She sighed contentedly, a sleepy smile tipping up the sides of her lips.

"Lean back, so I can wash your hair." Giving him a grateful nod, Holera tilted her head back and closed her eyes as Kason's skilled hands began to work the fragrant soap through her temporarily black tresses. She was beautiful with any color of hair, but he couldn't wait to remove the darkness and bring the platinum of her natural hair back out.

"What do you think we'll find in those caves?" she asked, her voice barely audible above the trickle of water as he rinsed her hair with a mug of water. "What do you think of the merchants' tale? The magic they spoke of could be potent enough to turn tides."

"Who knows? Stories are like the sea—both hold secrets beneath their surfaces." Leaning forward, he lathered his hands with soap and smoothed them along her curves, needing to touch her more than he needed his next breath. "But one thing is certain, my fierce warrior: investigating this further, especially under the nose of the king, could pose great danger. We must be cautious. Although I know it's necessary, I don't like putting you into these perilous situations."

Holera hummed in agreement, her eyes opening to meet his gaze. "Promise me, Kason," she whispered, holding his hand on her stomach with her own. "Promise me that we'll make it back home after this. Settle down and live our lives for ourselves for a while."

The vulnerability in her eyes was something Holera rarely showed, not to anyone but him. His heart swelled with emotion, his hands cradling her face as he pressed a tender kiss to her lips. "I promise you this and so much more, my mate. I told you, I'm putting a child in you after this—if that's something you want as well."

She reached up, her hand clasping his on her cheek. "It's a future we can both dream about until we can make it come true."

As Holera emerged from the bath, her skin glistening like moonlight on waves, Kason prepared his own. He sank into the tub, muscles easing as the heat seeped into his bones. Holera, perched on a stool beside him, traced patterns in the condensation on the stone walls, her thoughts seemingly as fluid as the ripples she drew.

"Tomorrow we should blend in with the market crowds, listen to the gossip. If the caves hide treasures, someone's tongue will be loose enough to guide us," she mused, her gaze flitting to Kason's inked skin, where a massive phoenix coiled around his arm and onto his chest—an image he'd had made permanent on his skin the moment she'd accepted him as her mate. Holera was a stunning female, the most breathtaking in all of Ekotoria, but her phoenix form was absolutely majestic—a true work of art that could never be duplicated.

"Agreed," he affirmed, submerging deeper, letting the water rise to his shoulders. "But when night falls, we'll take to the cliffs."

Skin still flushed and slightly damp from the bath, Kason guided Holera to the bed with tender reverence, his hands tracing the contours of her shoulders before easing her down onto the soft expanse of the quilt. They were both tired, but he'd waited all day to touch her, and it had been a day too long.

Starting at her forehead, Kason's lips pressed a trail of fervent devotion on Holera's body, stopping at her lips as he dragged his cock against her center. Their kisses were deep, hungry, as if each moment might be their last. His hands explored every inch of her, memorizing the curves he knew so well, as if they had been carved into his very soul. As her fingers raked down his back, his mouth wandered down, lingering at the hollow of her throat where her pulse beat a rhythm akin to his own. When he reached the valley between her breasts and lavished attention to her nipples, she arched off the bed, a gasp leaving her lips. With her fingers threading into his hair, she rolled her hips, only encouraging his descent further.

Submitting to her unspoken demands, he kissed and licked his way down her stomach, drawing closer to the apex of her thighs, where her essence beckoned him like a siren song. With his hand on her knee, he spread her legs open for him, taking her in for a few slow heartbeats that only made his cock grow painfully harder. His tongue danced over her clitoris, a flicker one moment, a slow, sensual drag the next, that had her grinding against his face. The taste of her brought a rumble from his chest, stoking flames inside his core that he knew reflected what burned inside hers.

Slipping his finger inside her, he rubbed the sensitive spot on her inner wall, knowing exactly what it took to make his mate shatter into pieces. And shatter she did.

Climax hitting her like the waves crashing outside their window, Holera's body tensed around him, a moan leaving her lips as the taste coated his tongue. He kissed and licked her through her orgasm, savoring every drop of her arousal until she was limp on the bed—pliable and ready to take all of him.

"You are so beautiful," he said as he pulled her close to his chest, her legs wrapping around his waist as he flipped them over. "I could look at you like this all the days of my life and never desire another view."

Eyes glazed by lust, Holera guided her hand to his throbbing cock, positioning it at her entrance. Her touch was almost too much to bear, but he held on, his restraint hanging on by the thinnest of threads. "You're not so bad yourself."

They both groaned as she slid down onto him, the wet warmth of her body welcoming him like it was made for him, because it was. The scent of their arousal mingled with the sea air, crashing waves outside echoing the pounding of their hearts. Every kiss and breath they shared deepened the love between them, filling Kason's heart until it felt like it may burst.

With his hands gripping her perfect backside, Kason's thrusts became more urgent, more demanding, as he claimed her completely, every inch of him belonging to her and only her. He was lost in her, drowning in the perfection of her body, the way she felt wrapped around him like a second skin. Her nails clawed at his flesh, the sting of pain only spurring him on, heightening the pleasure beyond anything he'd ever known before her. Time didn't exist before her.

Their climaxes hit like a tempest, a maelstrom of sensation that ripped through them like a force of nature. Wave after wave of ecstasy crashed over them, the pleasure so intense it left them both gasping for breath, their bodies intertwined in a tangled mass of limbs and sheets.

As the tremors subsided and Holera lay there panting heavily on top of him, her heart hammering against his own, Kason couldn't help but marvel at the depth of his love for this female. She was his compass star, his guiding light in the darkest of times. And in that moment, he knew that as long as they were together, they could face any storm and emerge stronger for it.

Chapter Thirteen

Aurelia

The sun dipped low on the horizon, casting a brilliant spectrum of colors over the sapphire waters of the Irriboia Sea as the ship cut through the waves. The vessel groaned beneath them, its timbers creaking like old bones, as if the sea itself was listening for secrets carried on the wind. They had been aboard for less than a day, having just barely escaped the port town after being attacked by rebels.

In the candlelit quarters of the healer, Alteria, Rockie, and Nikoleta lay side by side on narrow cots—Rockie with a severe gash on her left arm, and Nikoleta with a broken collarbone and an arrow wound in her thigh. The scent of healing herbs filled the air, mingling with the salty sea breeze that filtered through the open porthole.

"Try to relax," murmured Alteria, her skilled hands weaving magical threads that danced around Rockie's wounded arm. Although fae healed quickly, magic in Ekotoria had become unpredictable since the portal's destruction, preventing many from using their powers as they once had. Each spark of Alteria's weaving flickered like a candle threatened by a draft, proof that even the most reliable powers had grown uncertain.

"Thank you," Rockie whispered through gritted teeth, sweat beading on her brow. Nikoleta, ever the stoic Aegrician warrior, simply nodded, her jaw clenched as Alteria rewrapped her shoulder.

From the shadowed corridor, Aurelia and Cristos entered through the narrow doorway. Cristos leaned against the frame while Aurelia stepped closer, concern etched on her face. "Is there anything we can do to help?"

"Your presence is already a comfort, my queen," Alteria replied with a hint of a smile. "They will recover soon enough. For now, they just need rest."

"Thank you for taking such good care of our friends," Cristos said, resting a hand on Aurelia's shoulder.

"Of course, my king. It is my duty and honor." With a respectful dip of her chin, Alteria turned back to her patients, lifting a glass of water to Rockie's lips.

With one last look at the injured warriors, Aurelia and Cristos made their way back above deck, where Bremusa, Septima, Exie, and Vasilis were waiting for them.

Back above deck, where the sky stretched vast and endless, Aurelia and her council gathered near the ship's railing, the setting sun casting a golden glow over the horizon. Surrounded by loyalty, Aurelia felt the weight of responsibility settle upon her like iron upon her skull. If only Otera, Blaedia, and Taryn had been there as well, but she trusted them to look after Aegricia while she was gone. She only hoped the earthquake they had felt in Spectre Forest hadn't originated from Flamecliff.

"Tell us about the Inferno Territories," Aurelia said, directing her question to Bremusa, the eldest member of their group. "What should we expect when we arrive?"

Bremusa gazed out at the horizon as if she could see the territories in the distance, the sunset reflecting in her silver eyes. "The Inferno Territories consist of many islands and three kingdoms on the main continent. However, we must tread carefully, distinguishing allies from those who would seek to harm us. Monarchs can be fickle, and many have powerful mages at their sides. The power of the portal pulls me in this direction, but that doesn't mean we aren't sailing into a trap."

Her words were as steady as the sea, yet an undertow of dread pulled Aurelia into cold depths.

Amidst the many pressing priorities on her mind, she couldn't ignore her worsening morning sickness, which had transformed into nearly all-day discomfort since boarding the Siren Song. Thankfully, Kassandra had packed herbs in her satchel, and she had already had to ask the ship's cook, Cisseus, to prepare tea multiple times.

"Do you think the Shadow Glass was used to divert the portal away from us?" Cristos asked, wrapping his arm around Aurelia to steady her as the ship rocked. "Is that even possible—that someone could have had the foresight to do that?"

Without hesitation, Bremusa nodded. "We would be foolish to think otherwise. If I can sense its power, others can as well. I do not know of any of my kind still existing in this world, but whispers on the wind hint that they are out there."

Raised in the human realm, Aurelia knew little about creatures like Bremusa—*elementals*—but the warning in Bremusa's tone made her skin crawl. There was so much she needed to learn about her new world and its inhabitants if she was to lead them successfully.

"Can you tell us more about the specific kingdoms?" she asked, leaning back against Cristos' chest. He wrapped his arm around her waist, his warmth soothing the anxious knot within her.

"We can consult the most recent map," Vasilis suggested, speaking up for the first time. Being from Norithae, he wasn't someone Aurelia knew well. Still, Cristos had grown up with him, making the winged male a valuable member of their group. "The map we have is from a recent diplomatic mission. It should be accurate, although it doesn't include all the smaller islands."

In the dim glow of oil lamps swaying with the gentle motion of the ship, Aurelia, Cristos, and the others huddled over the expansive map spread across the oaken table in their quarters. The Inferno Territories sprawled before them—a tapestry of potential alliances and lurking dangers, each kingdom a piece of the puzzle they needed to solve.

Bremusa leaned in, her silver eyes catching the lamplight as she traced the borders with a slender finger. "Here," she said, pointing to one of the larger outlines on the main continent. "Cineris, with its ash-veiled mountains, is probably as far north as we can go by land. King Damianos has supported our monarchy for centuries, but we must beware of the shadow creatures that haunt Cineris' mountain passes, along with the stories of powerful mages who control them. They can be dangerous—soul-sucking."

Aurelia pictured faceless wraiths clinging to the mountains, feeding on every fragile dream.

"Shadow creatures?" Septima repeated, stepping closer to Exie. Her deep brown gaze flickered to the dark corners of the room as if expecting ethereal foes to emerge from the shadows.

"More myth than menace," Vasilis interjected, his fingers dancing across the charted waters just beyond the territories, where serpentine lines marked treacherous currents. "Yet myths often bear truth, especially here, where the veil between worlds is thin."

"Thin enough for a portal, perhaps?" Cristos asked, gently squeezing Aurelia's shoulder.

"Indeed," Bremusa responded, her smile as enigmatic as ever. "But not necessarily the portal we're looking for. There are false portals—those that reflect our deepest desires and darkest fears—portals we would hope to never stumble into."

Just the thought of such a portal sent a shiver down Aurelia's spine and turned her stomach. "And this kingdom?" Aurelia asked, pointing to the northernmost tip of the continent, which was colored nearly all in black.

"The Scorched Realm," Bremusa said, her tone revealing far more than her words. "It's as fierce as its name suggests. Fire mages rule there, their power drawn from the volcanoes that scar the land. There is no monarch, but a sorceress—Zervia. I knew her once—long before I found my way to Aegricia and became the closest friend of your mother."

The comment took Aurelia by surprise, her heart flipping. "My mother?"

Bremusa nodded, her sharp features softening. "Messalina and I were the closest of friends before she fled Aegricia, and I became the advisor and confidant of her sister." She huffed out a laugh, her silver eyes growing distant. "She and I were like sisters—always getting into one thing or another—while Otera was forced by your great-grandmother to entertain the court. Both sisters hated it, but Messalina always found a way to escape her grandmother's near-constant parading."

The memory softened Bremusa's silver eyes, and Aurelia caught a glimpse not of the elemental but of the girl her mother had once laughed beside.

Even as a smile spread across her lips, longing filled Aurelia's heart. Bremusa's admission made her want to know her even more—not as an elemental, but as the keeper of her mother's memory. After so many years without her, Aurelia craved every scrap of Messalina she could find.

Stepping around the table, Septima moved closer to Aurelia and reached for her hand. "Our mother had a rebellious spirit."

Aurelia's old friend dipped her chin, a smile spreading across her lips. "Indeed, she did."

Pushing the memories aside, Aurelia cleared her throat. "What about the other kingdoms? Where will we first make land in the Inferno Territories?"

Vasilis leaned over the table and traced a line southward to where the sea met the shores, the land depicted in a brilliant shade of green. "We are likely to touch land at the Emerald Enclave in a few days. It's shrouded in perpetual mist and is said to be home to elusive nature spirits."

All eyes turned to Bremusa, who could be considered a nature spirit herself. "Queen Thesipha is a dryad—a forest nymph. If the portal has appeared on her lands, she will undoubtedly want to see it gone. The last thing she desires is war there. Bloodshed would tarnish her land and destroy everything she and her people cherish. We already know the lengths some would go to in order to control access to the human world. No matter where this portal manifests, it will draw conflict."

Aurelia's gaze drifted to the map's green expanse, wondering if the misty forests would welcome them or swallow them whole.

Chapter Fourteen

Taryn

The once bustling harbor of Flamecliff lay in ruins, its splendor snuffed out like a candle in a tempest. Taryn's heart thundered in her chest, a relentless drumbeat as she wove through the chaos with the grace of the mythical phoenix she harbored within. Broken statues lay shattered in the streets, scattered like discarded toys. The harbor, usually teeming with activity, now resembled a graveyard of splintered wood and twisted metal, the carcasses of mighty ships beached like so many whales. The sea's retreat had left scars in the earth itself, as though the waves had clawed away the city's soul before abandoning it. Her eyes, reflecting the fiery hues of the sun that had risen after the tsunami washed away the bloodstains of war, yet left destruction in its wake, scanned the wreckage, seeking signs of life amidst the desolation.

"Otera! Blaedia!" she called out, her voice slicing through the cries of the injured.

"Over here!" From the other side of the washed-out street, Otera's red hair appeared, Blaedia beside her with a young female in her arms. As Blaedia rushed past her, heading for the infirmary tent further down the street, Otera pulled Taryn into a hug.

"I'm so glad you're okay!" the former queen said, relief filling her voice. "We are so lucky this area wasn't busy when the water came in, but keep looking for anyone who may be hurt."

Taryn nodded, rubbing Otera's back before pulling away to look amongst the rubble.

"Taryn!" The desperate call pierced through the destruction, seizing Taryn's soul. Heart leaping in her throat, she spun around.

Through the haze emerged a winged figure, Lars' strides as frantic as a storm-chased sailor. In his eyes burned a desperation that mirrored her own, an unspoken prayer that neither had lost the other to water or ruin. Their eyes met across the distance, twin oceans of emotion crashing into one another. With every step he took, the weight of worry lifted from her shoulders until he was close enough for her to see the glistening tracks of tears on his worried face.

"Taryn!" he cried again, his voice ragged with relief, and she flew into his arms, the force of their embrace a testament to the affection that had blossomed between them in the shadow of loss. She sank into his arms as they encircled her, allowing him to pull her in.

"By all the stars, I thought I'd lost you," he whispered into her hair, his breath hot against her scalp. "When I felt the ground shake... saw the water rise..."

"Never that easy to get rid of me." She smiled, the light-heartedness of her words belying the tremor that shook her frame. But it was true—after everything that had happened in recent days, it seemed as though the veil wasn't ready to take her yet.

They pulled back just enough to look into each other's eyes, finding comfort when the world seemed intent on rending itself apart.

"Come," Taryn said, reaching out to take his hand. "We have work to do."

Her voice carried not just urgency but defiance, a vow that grief would not be the only thing to define her.

For the next several hours, Taryn and Lars joined those who were uninjured as they looked for survivors and helped those who needed it. Otera had been right when she'd said they were lucky with the timing. Since the war had only just ended, many of Aegricia's citizens were still outside the city in camps, leaving a tiny percentage of the populace in the area near the harbor. There were still many injured, but so many fewer than there could have been.

Once the injured had been tended to, Taryn and Lars went to the palace to help with meal preparation and distribution. As the sun set over the Elder Sea, draping the broken harbor in a blanket of darkness, they were both exhausted. For a moment, once everything had gone quiet, Taryn glanced down the street where she knew her home still stood, debating if she should attempt to spend the night there. But after only that moment, she decided against it, realizing she would probably never be able to return there again—not with the ghost of Cassius still there. Just the thought of his scent lingering on the sheets sent tears that burned the backs of her eyes. The memory of him clung like smoke, impossible to banish, choking even in the quiet. She turned away, blowing out a breath as she willed the emotion to return to the shadowed corners of her heart, where she could put up walls to keep them right where she wanted them.

"Are you okay?" Lars' smooth voice cut through the misery of her thoughts, pulling her attention. "Can I do something to help you, Taryn? If there's anything I can do, ju—"

Before he could finish, she wrapped her arms around his neck, pulling her lips to his in a desperate kiss. "If you want to make me feel better," she whispered against his lips, her voice trembling, "I need your cock inside me."

Lars' eyes widened, and he chuckled, mischief twisting his lips. Without another word, he scooped Taryn up into his arms, his massive bat wings unfurling behind him. They took off into the sky, leaving the city far behind as they soared over the sea.

With her legs wrapped around his waist, Taryn clung to Lars as they flew higher and faster, the cool wind whipping through her long hair. Even with the brine of the water beneath them, all she could smell was Lars' scent, woodsy and fresh, intoxicating. Threading her fingers into his long brown hair, she pulled his face to hers, tracing his lips with her tongue. "This is fun and all, but I asked for your cock to be inside me."

He grinned, the look purely wicked as he flipped her around in the air in front of him, pulling her until her back was against his chest, his massive wings sending them higher into the clouds.

"Then take off your trousers." The way his breath coasted against her neck as he gave the order sent warm wetness between her thighs.

Taking not even a moment to think, she unclasped her trousers as his arms held her in front of him. The air from his wingbeats fluttered against her naked flesh, only turning her on more. When her trousers were tucked safely into the satchel over her shoulder, she reached between them, finding his stiff cock already freed from his clothing, the tip dripping with precum as she gripped it.

"Are you ready for me to put that inside your pretty cunt?"

Taryn looked around, the sky dark aside from the crescent moon and a million stars, but she could tell they were very high up, which made her a little uneasy without her wings. She'd never been so high without her own phoenix form to keep her safe. "You—uh—want to do this here?"

Without saying a word, Lars lifted her slightly, wrapping his hands around her waist and thrusting into her from behind, all the way to the hilt. A moment later, they were soaring through the air as Lars held onto her hips, thrusting into her without restraint.

"Scream to the stars, Taryn. Tell them how good it feels to have me so deep inside you while your life is in my hands."

And when she did, her cry scattered into the night sky like sparks, as though the heavens themselves bore witness to their joining. The thrill of their lovemaking in the air was intoxicating, each thrust driving away the darkness that lingered in her heart.

"Harder," Taryn gasped, her body arching against his, urging him to take her with all he had.

"Are you sure?" Lars panted, clearly holding back.

"Please," she insisted, her nails digging into his muscular thighs as she sought release from the turmoil within her.

Lars obliged, his wings beating powerfully as he took them higher still, their bodies moving together in a passionate dance that defied gravity. When their climaxes hit, the world fell away as they screamed their orgasms to the stars and moon.

Something at that moment clicked into place that she'd thought had clicked for her a long time ago—something that only happened once in someone's lifetime: a mating bond. It was not chosen, not sought, yet it was rooted in her bones with a certainty that terrified her as much as it steadied her.

In the heart of the palace's grand hall, rays of sunlight filtered through the stained-glass windows, casting a kaleidoscope of colors upon Taryn's face as she studied the map spread out before her. Lars stood beside her, with Otera and Blaedia across the table. The weight of the decisions they had to make bore down on her like a dragon perched on her shoulders.

"Moving people inland is our best bet," Blaedia said, her fingers tracing the path southward from Flamecliff to Spectre Forest.

"Agreed," Otera replied, her voice decisive, like the queen she'd been for decades. "I cannot bear the thought of more suffering because we failed to act." For a moment, the former queen went silent, sadness darkening her features. "We've already lost so much."

Taryn dipped her chin, knowing precisely what had crossed the queen's mind when the shadows moved across her eyes. Not only had they lost people, but she and the former queen had also lost their lives. If the portal hadn't been destroyed, dispersing its magic across their world, they would both still be dead. "There is a large clearing not far from the Norithae camp in Spectre Forest. That would be a good location. It is a few miles away from the coast."

"Then it's settled," Otera said, tapping her finger on the map. "We will begin the relocation immediately. Gather volunteers, supplies—anything necessary to create a sanctuary for our people in Spectre Forest."

With their meeting over, Taryn and Lars wasted no time organizing the relocation efforts, utilizing those who were able-bodied to pack up horse-drawn carts with all the supplies they needed. She didn't know how long their people would need to stay away from the city—disrupting their daily lives—but their safety was of the utmost importance. Some would need to spend their days in the city to help with rebuilding and cleanup efforts, but those who were not required in the city, like the elderly and children, could remain in the camp until their capital was safe once again.

As night fell, the once-empty clearing boomed into a thriving camp, filled with the sounds of laughter and camaraderie. Taryn watched as children played among the tents, their imaginations transforming them into phoenixes soaring above the sea. In that moment, she allowed herself to hope that they were forging a brighter future for all. "We're making progress, but there's still so much to do."

"Take it one day at a time," Lars said, wrapping his arm around Taryn's waist and pulling her against his body. "Even the mightiest statues begin as mere lumps of clay. Just like the phoenixes they are, your people will rise from the ashes. We will rebuild, and we will be stronger for it."

"Thank you," she whispered, leaning into his touch, her mind still reeling from the undeniable sensation she'd experienced the night before—the mating bond that had fallen into place between them. They hadn't talked about it afterward, both too exhausted when they arrived back at the Norithae camp, but she had no doubt Lars had felt it too. Even though she knew fate controlled the bond shared by true mates, and that it wasn't a decision she'd made herself, it still filled her with more guilt for the male she'd only just lost—the male she'd spent so many years of her life with. Her heart mourned him, and probably would for the rest of her life, but everything else in her life was too confusing to grieve, at least for now. One day, when the world grew quiet, the loss of Cassius would hit her like a tsunami that had wreaked havoc on her beloved city, and when that time came, she would have no choice but to open the floodgates.

But for now, she clung to the fragile present, knowing storms could be postponed but never denied.

Chapter Fifteen

Kason

Sunlight filtered through the curtains, causing Holera's silver hair to shimmer as she lay draped across Kason's larger frame. The morning air was filled with the tantalizing scent of freshly baked bread and the distant hum of the market, gently pulling them from their slumber. Kason opened his eyes to find Holera gazing back at him, her expression filled with love and warmth.

"Good morning, my phoenix," he murmured, brushing a strand of hair from her face and kissing her forehead. "Are you ready for today's adventure?"

With a lazy stretch that made her silver waves ripple across the pillow, Holera let out a contented sigh. "Always."

As they climbed out of bed, they dressed for the day ahead in outfits that would help them blend in with the townsfolk. Kason chose a tunic that matched the sea's azure, while Holera opted for a simple dress that fluttered with each movement. Though she grumbled the entire time about wearing a dress, Kason couldn't take his eyes off her. The violet dress accentuated every one of her curves, and he looked forward to removing it from her body that night.

Leaving the tavern shortly after breakfast, they ventured into the bustling market, the vibrant colors and enticing scents enveloping them like a warm embrace. Hand-in-hand, they meandered through the stalls, eavesdropping on conversations between merchants and shoppers, hoping to glean further information on the coastal caves. The market's noise was a cloak and a curse—its chatter thick enough to conceal their presence, yet thin enough to hide whispers worth dying for.

For several hours, they wandered around the market, sampling the local delicacies and inhaling the scents of exotic spices and fresh fruits. Their keen ears picked up snippets of conversations, but most were about mundane things.

They sauntered down the pier, pretending to be a mated couple merely on a stroll. With the day's catch being unloaded and merchants preparing ships, there were many lingering near the harbor. Kason knew how much sailors loved to share tall tales, so he hoped they could overhear something of use near the water.

"Did these come from the caves?" one merchant asked another as they haggled over the price of a magical trinket. Waiting for the response, Kason and Holera stopped walking. Hoping not to appear like eavesdroppers, Kason wrapped his arms around his mate, pulling her into a kiss. She didn't resist, sliding her fingers into his hair as she slid her tongue into his mouth.

"Rumors, mostly," the other merchant replied, his voice skeptical. Unable to help himself, Kason kissed Holera deeper, the taste of her stiffening his cock in his trousers and making it difficult to pay attention. "But if they hold even a fraction of the treasures people claim, it would be worth the risk."

"Are you going to go and take care of your woman, or does someone else need to do it?" a gruff voice said from behind them. Kason's head snapped to the side, his arms pulling Holera even closer. Behind them, one of the merchants was watching, his hand palming his cock through his trousers. The lewd gesture was as dangerous as a blade, for it tempted Kason to break their cover with blood.

Kason snarled, reaching for his blade, but Holera wrapped her hand around his, stopping him. With a sneer at the merchant, whose greasy hair hung in knotted clumps around his face, Holera slid her arm around Kason's back, pulling his attention back to her. "Let's go back to the room, killer, so instead of beating him down, you can take all that rage out on my cunt."

Stepping away from the pier, Holera led Kason back toward the tavern, his blood still boiling from the merchant's behavior. He wanted nothing more than to beat the male's face in, but his mate came first.

The moment they reached their room above the tavern, Kason lifted Holera, her legs wrapping around his waist as he pressed her against the wall.

"You should have let me hit him," he growled, unclasping his trousers.

Holera kissed him wildly, her words broken between kisses. "We can't afford to draw attention to ourselves."

Harder than it had ever been, Kason's cock sprang free. Not bothering to remove her undergarments, he hooked his finger into them, nudging them aside as he thrusted up into her.

A groan tore from them both when he drove in to the hilt, the warmth of her body consuming him like an inferno.

"Your beauty already draws attention, my fierce warrior," he said, thrusting into her with a brutal cadence. "And your scent—gods, you smell delicious."

The obscene, wet sounds of their coupling echoed through the hall. Gripping her hips to angle her just the way he wanted, Kason surged into her with unrestrained passion. Every stroke was a promise of possession, a proclamation of love, and an oath of protection. Her nails dug into his back, her body pulsating in rhythm with his.

For a moment, Kason forgot about the vile merchant by the docks and about their mission altogether. It was just the two of them, as it always would be. But after he brought his mate to the clouds and they sank to the floor sweaty, boneless, and sated, their obligations were still waiting.

Clad in the darkness of night, Kason and Holera emerged from the back door of the inn, their black cloaks billowing like the sails of phantom ships setting a course for uncharted waters. Every shadow felt alive, stretching long fingers toward them as if to warn them back. The moon hung overhead, a silent sentinel casting its pale glow upon the towers of the palace that loomed in the distance.

"Ready?" Kason asked, his voice barely audible over the sounds of music and revelry still drifting from the tavern.

With a gleam in her dark eyes that reflected the stars, Holera nodded. "Always."

Taking to the back alleys, they walked hand-in-hand, their weapons hidden beneath their cloaks as they made their way toward the sea. Being a coastal city, Embershell was bordered by the sea on two sides, with only one road leading in and out. To avoid drawing attention, they headed for the cliffs.

Reaching the far end of the silent beach, Kason pulled her close. "If we see even a hint of a dragon, we halt our mission for the night. Nothing is worth putting you in danger."

Holera kissed his neck softly. "That's something I can agree with."

With one more kiss, Holera shifted, her silhouette transforming into a majestic phoenix. Her feathers shimmered like quicksilver in the moonlight. Sliding onto her back, Kason felt a surge of power as they launched into the sky.

The southern coast of the continent was framed by jagged cliffs and rock formations—countless hiding places carved by the sea. Kason scanned the cliffs, searching for openings large enough to conceal the trade of priceless artifacts.

Then he saw it—a massive shadow heading straight for them. Holera veered sharply toward the cliffs, plunging into the gaping mouth of a cave.

The cave's entrance yawned wide, a dark maw ready to swallow them whole. The air inside was damp and metallic, with a faint, lingering taste of secrets too long buried. Holera touched down on the jagged terrain with grace, shifting back into her fae form as Kason kept a watchful eye on the skies.

Satisfied that they were alone, Kason lit a torch, the flame flickering as shadows receded. Stalagmites rose like guardians around them, protecting secrets older than the merfolk who called Diapolis home.

Kason and Holera walked for what felt like hours, their hope dimming like the flickering light of a torch against the oppressive darkness. Just as doubt began to seep into Kason's resolve, they entered a grotto aglow with coral that hummed with magic, its luminescence a tapestry of aqua and emerald hues. The light pulsed as if the cavern itself were drawing breath, a living witness to their presence.

Kason reached for Holera's hand, the sight stealing his breath away.

"How?" Holera whispered, awe evident in her voice.

Equally entranced, Kason kissed her hair. "I don't know, but experiencing this with you makes it even more special."

"Do you think anyone knows this is here?"

Kason shrugged, rubbing her knuckles. "If they do, I hope they forget about it—at least for tonight."

The air was thick with enchantment, and it didn't take long before the grotto ensnared them. It was as if the grotto demanded tribute, weaving their bodies closer until love itself became an offering. They discarded their garments and stepped into the water, its warmth feeling like a lover's touch. With skin as smooth as satin beneath his hands, Kason pulled Holera close, her violet eyes shimmering in the ethereal light. His lips found hers, and passion rose like the tide.

"Kason," Holera gasped, her voice a plea. "I need you. Now."

"I need you, my fierce warrior. Forever."

Their union sparked the cavern alive. The luminescent coral flickered like stars, as if responding to their joining. No words could capture the flood of devotion coursing through Kason as he met her movements thrust for thrust, their beings intertwining until climax tore through them, the soul of the grotto joining in a release that transcended flesh.

As their shared rapture ebbed into tenderness, they remained locked together, knowing they had created something more wondrous than any artifact could be. In that moment, Kason wondered if they had uncovered not just treasure, but a prophecy written in flesh and light.

Chapter Sixteen

Variel

The scent of earth was strong beneath Variel's paws, a rich blend of pine needles and damp soil invading her heightened senses. She moved silently through the dense underbrush of the human realm, the sleek black fur of her wolf form blending with the darkness of the forest under the crescent moon. Muscles rippled beneath her coat, every fiber of her being attuned to the faintest sign of Joneira or the elusive portal they both sought as she navigated the rugged terrain. Each step pressed into ground that felt more like a battlefield than soil.

The oracle's intuition guided her movements, a gift of foresight flickering in her mind as if an invisible thread connected her to her fate. They had already been trapped in the human realm for three days, and there was still no sign of a way back home or of their enemies since leaving the site of their awakening.

Her dark eyes glowed in the moonlight, scanning the surroundings for any disturbance—a broken branch, a scrap of fabric caught in thorns—anything that might reveal where her enemies had gone. Her lupine ears twitched at every sound, sorting through the hoots of owls and the scurrying of rodents, searching for presences that didn't belong.

Moving like a specter, she slipped past the outskirts of a small human settlement, where laughter and firelight spilled into the night. Variel knew well the dangers of crossing paths with humans, who would kill her the moment they spotted her, so she did her best to stay out of their way. Instead, the shadows became her allies, and she their willing accomplice, gliding through the night unseen and unheard, yet ever present. The laughter of humans echoed behind her like a foreign song, reminding her that she was a ghost in their world—just one misstep away from peril.

A mile deeper into the forest, where the unstable portal had left them behind, the scent of charred earth and the tang of blood still hung heavily in the air. Trees stood like wounded sentinels, their bark bearing witness to the events that had transpired there, but there was no sign of the others—no sign of Joneira—no sign of a way back home. The portal, along with her enemies, was gone.

With near-silent footsteps, her senses pulled her along the winding path toward a large river that cut through the landscape. For a while, she walked beside it, but as the river broadened, the scent she pursued became fainter, diluted by the fresh water in the breeze until it vanished altogether. The current sang a siren's song, tempting her to slip beneath its surface, but Variel knew better than to enter. With the strength of its current, the river could wash away more than just a scent. Not finding what she sought should have deterred her, but determination coiled within her like a spring, compelling her to veer away from the water's edge, her eyes scanning the wilderness for any other signs she may have missed.

The human realm she found herself in was a cacophony of new sights and sounds, an orchestra created by the rustling leaves and the distant calls of unfamiliar creatures. A family of deer emerged from the underbrush, their movements tentative and watchful. In the fae realm, such creatures bore the spirits of the ancients, whispering the secrets of the forest. Here, however, they were merely prey, caught in the relentless cycle of life and death—a harsh reminder of the human realm's raw simplicity.

A rabbit dashed across her path, its heartbeat a frantic drumbeat against the stillness of the night. Recognizing the panic in its eyes, she allowed it to continue on its way, at least for the moment.

As she wove through the endless foliage of the untamed forest, Variel's steps slowed when an anomaly in the landscape caught her attention. A tangle of vines and moss cloaked a jagged opening in the hillside—an entrance to a hidden world below.

Watching the opening for a moment, she shifted her weight, the pads of her paws pressing into the soft soil as the dark cave beckoned her closer. She knew that entering it was risky, but her desperate need to find a way back home pushed her forward. With a cautious step and heightened senses, she stepped into the opening.

Inside, the darkness felt alive, waiting and watching. Variel shrugged off the unsettling sensation. The air clung damp against her fur, thick with secrets that hadn't seen daylight in centuries. Still in her wolf form, her eyes adjusted to the lack of light, revealing a tapestry of symbols etched into the rocky walls.

The markings were both foreign and familiar, like a song from a half-remembered dream. Although she couldn't read them, she could feel their significance, or at least she believed so. Tracing a claw across one of the glyphs, a surge of ancient energy reverberated through her, sending a shiver down her spine. It was as if she were touching the heartbeat of the earth itself, a rhythm older than the divide between realms. Each symbol seemed to be part of a larger puzzle, a map leading to the secrets that could either bridge realms or destroy them.

Staring at the walls before her, Variel's mind raced. Could these markings be remnants of a time long ago when humans and fae walked side by side? Or perhaps they were a key left by the creators of the universe to unlock the path home? Or were they merely the carvings of a primitive society that knew nothing of the world?

As Variel stood inside the main chamber, the fur on the back of her neck rose, a tickling sensation that sent a clear signal of approaching danger. Pressing herself against the cool stone wall, she felt the shadows wrap around her like a cloak. The damp, earthy scent of wet stone filled her nostrils as she squeezed her eyes shut, concentrating on the sounds that pricked at her ears.

Footsteps—measured and deliberate—approached the mouth of the cave, the unmistakable sound of multiple boots drawing closer. Variel's heart quickened, the rhythm becoming an erratic drumbeat against the silence. Her instincts screamed at her to flee. She was a lone wolf, and there were several of them, yet she stood frozen, her form melting into the darkness of the cave's recesses. The cave seemed to tighten around her, as if the stone were conspiring with her fear.

Through the narrow slits of her eyes, she watched as four of Joneira's soldiers entered—her enemies, unaware of her presence. Although their faces were hidden in shadow, the scent of them and the gleam of their weapons were unmistakable. They were not human; they were warriors from the Inferno Territories.

"Spread out," one commanded in a low growl. "The queen said the portal's magic may linger somewhere in these mountains. We need to search everywhere."

"She will reward us handsomely if we find it first," another replied, greed dripping from his words.

Variel's pulse thudded in her ears, loud enough that she feared they might hear it. They were not just soldiers; they were hunters like her, seeking a prize that could tilt the balance of power. Her muscles tensed, ready to spring into action. Still, her mind held her back—she could not risk revealing herself and endangering her people.

As the warriors dispersed, their boots scraping against the stone floor, she inhaled deeply, memorizing their scents and voices. Holding her breath in the hope that they would not detect her, she crept along the cave's edge, silent as a serpent. Her thoughts raced, each heartbeat bringing her closer to a decision—whether to attack if they saw her or to flee.

"Imagine the chaos we could create with such power at our command," one warrior mused, malice twisting Variel's stomach.

"Power to bend the realms to our will," another added. His words slithered through the chamber like venom, poisoning the very air she breathed. Wondering if they planned to tell Joneira about their findings or if they aimed to harness the power for themselves, Variel realized that although they might lack the ability to control it, desperation rarely deterred ambitious seekers.

Their words struck a chord within Variel, igniting a fire that seared through her veins. She was engaged in more than just a quest for balance—it was a battle for the very soul of her world. If her enemies claimed the portal's power, everything she loved would be plunged into shadow and ruin.

Swallowing her trepidation, she slipped from one hiding spot to another, remaining in the shadows. The warriors' conversation faded into the background, their plans etched into her mind—a map of treachery she was determined to thwart. No matter what it took, she would find the portal first, protecting her world in the process. There was no other option. Failure was not an option—it meant extinction, and she would not allow her people to fade into myth.

Chapter Seventeen

Exie

Thunder cracked like a whip, tearing Exie from her dreams of sunnier days. She jolted awake, her heart pounding against her ribs as another violent shudder rocked the ship. Beside her on the small bed, Septima groaned, sitting up with wide, alarmed eyes.

"What happened? What was that?" Septima asked, panic clear in her voice.

Exie slid out of bed and shoved her feet into her boots. "The sea is angry. Look for your sister—" She hesitated, leaning toward Septima as she dressed in her tunic. "Please stay below deck where it's safe."

Before Septima could argue, Exie dashed out of the room, heading above deck. She didn't look back to see if her stubborn mate had listened; she was sure she wouldn't.

Above deck, the scene was chaotic. In the darkness of night, rain lashed the timbers, and waves surged like sea monsters rising from the depths. Lightning stitched the sky from horizon to horizon, each bolt piercing open the sea's roar and turning the deck into a stage of fury.

Amid the tumultuous storm, Bremusa stood firm at the bow, her hands outstretched as if she could control the water. Exie wasn't sure of the limits of the ancient elemental's power, but she knew that a powerful warding spell could help—at least a little. Her mind raced, mapping the ship in an instant—mast, lines, crew, Septima—triage wrapped in strategy, because panic helped no one.

"Exie!" Cristos yelled from the mast, where he was helping the crew with the sails. "We need all hands!"

Darting across the deck, Exie grabbed the rope, her muscles straining as she fought to stabilize the mast. It sent her heart into her stomach when Septima rushed up behind her, reaching for the ropes as well.

"Keep her steady!" Vasilis roared above the noise, aiding the captain in steering the wheel with the tenacity of a seasoned mariner, his eyes fixed on an unseen horizon beyond the storm's veil.

"Exie!" a voice called from somewhere behind her. "I need your help to create a shield!"

It only took Exie a moment to realize it was Bremusa summoning her.

As the vessel heaved beneath them, Exie and Bremusa stood shoulder to shoulder, sheets of rain soaking through their clothing. With her heart thundering in time with the celestial clash above, Bremusa extended her hands, palms facing the tempest's wrath. Exie's blonde hair, pulled back into a long braid, whipped in the violent wind as she mirrored the gesture. Together, they summoned the essence of Exie's phoenix lineage and Bremusa's elemental power—a swirling vortex of flames that danced at their command. Their magics intertwined like braided fire, neither overtaking the other, stronger for the union.

"By the fire reborn," Exie cried out, invoking the ancestral mantra. Heat surged within her at the words, an inferno waiting to be unleashed.

"Let our protection be as the eternal sun," Bremusa added, her voice strong against the howling wind.

A burst of fire erupted from their joined hands, spiraling upwards. It unfurled like the wings of a mighty phoenix, enveloping the ship in a cocoon of protection that miraculously did not burn it. Heat licked their cheeks without burning, a living veil that turned rain to steam and force into harmless mist. The fiery shield, undulating with each roll of the ship, held back the torrential fury, diverting the vengeful spears of water that sought to claim them for the depths.

The crew watched in awe as the sea's chill was replaced by the warmth of the phoenix's fire. In the glow of the fiery dome, faces etched with exhaustion were briefly illuminated with hope, their fears reduced to mere embers flickering in the night.

Yet, as the maelstrom raged on, a cold shiver ran through Exie's veins, extinguishing her momentary triumph. The ghosts of her past flooded into her mind, threatening to overcome her with memories. She saw it again—the harbor of Flamecliff, the destruction, the day she lost her mate. The scalding memory seared her heart anew as her new mate stood braced against the mast of a violently rocking ship in the middle of a stormy sea. She knew she wouldn't survive losing this love. She tasted iron at the back of her throat as the sorrow bubbled up, forcing it down with the stubbornness that had kept her alive.

The tempest howled its ancient fury, transforming the ship into a mere plaything in the grasp of an enraged sea. Exie's heart beat a frantic rhythm against her rib cage, each thump echoing the thunder outside. Amidst the chaos, a singular thought sliced through her fear: Septima. Her beloved, her mate, her heart's compass in this world.

"Exie!" Bremusa's sharp, urgent call pierced through the haunting visions, her hand squeezing Exie's tightly. "Stay with me! Hold the flame!"

Struggling against the swell of grief, Exie tightened her grasp on the present. She couldn't allow the specters of her memories to extinguish the fire that safeguarded those she loved.

As abruptly as it had begun, the storm's intensity faded. The waves, though still formidable, no longer sought to dominate the sky and the ship. The winds softened their mournful howl into a weary sigh, and the protective fire shield flickered, allowing Bremusa and Exie to let the magic fizzle out.

"Exie!"

Septima's voice cut through the lingering echoes of the storm, a siren's call sweeter than any melody. Exie's feet barely touched the deck as she sprinted toward her mate. The distance between them vanished in an instant, and they collided, both of their clothes soaked from the storm. Exie buried her face in the crook of Septima's neck, inhaling the salt that lingered on her skin. Her fingers traced an unspoken question along Septima's ribs, and the answer came in the form of a nod and a sigh that steadied Exie's pulse.

"Are you hurt?" she murmured, her hands roaming over Septima's back, searching for any injury.

Septima shook her head, rising onto her toes to give Exie a kiss. "I'm fine. We're both fine."

Around them, the ship groaned in relief, its timbers settling as if in gratitude to the warriors who had defended it. The sea's rage subsided to a begrudging calm, the last of the waves caressing the hull like a remorseful lover. High above, the clouds parted, allowing the stars to witness those who dared to weather the storm.

With the storm passing as quickly as it had set in, Exie wrapped her arm around her mate's waist and led her back below deck. After everything they'd just experienced and how much of her power had been drained, her hands still trembled, no matter how strong she was trying to be. She'd always been the warrior—the brave one—but at that moment, Septima stood taller. The sight did not unmake her; it remade her—two pillars sharing the same roof.

Back above deck, the crew was still getting the ship back into working order, but Cristos had already returned below deck as well, heading toward the healer's quarters, which was where Aurelia had remained during the storm. There was no doubt the new Aegrician queen would have been above deck with the rest of them if not for the future of their kingdom in her womb. Aurelia was more stubborn than her sister.

Arriving back at their small private quarters, Exie opened the door, closing it behind them. The moment they were alone, she pulled Septima against her body, their wet clothing dripping onto the wooden floorboards.

"I thought I was going to lose you." The words created physical pain inside Exie's chest, but they had to be said. The loss of Theoni was still a fresh wound on her heart—barely held together by roughly laid stitches—no matter how long it had been since her lover had died, and no matter how much she loved Septima.

"Wherever I go," Septima said, the candlelight reflecting in her dark gaze as she leaned closer and gave Exie a soft kiss on the mouth with those delectably full lips, "we're going together."

Exie nodded, kissing Septima again. "Well, the only place I want to take you for a long time is happy places... places where you won't have to wear drenched clothes."

Lifting a brow, Septima reached for the ties on Exie's tunic, pulling the knot loose. "We don't have to wear drenched clothes now."

Exie didn't resist as Septima lifted her tunic over her head, dropping the wet fabric to the ground. Her nipples pebbled in the cool air, her mate immediately wrapping her lips around one and sucking.

Heat flooded into Exie's core as Septima kissed her breast, her mate's other hand giving attention to the rest of her too-sensitive body. The storm's roll still moved through Exie's legs, a slow sway that met Septima's mouth and made the small room feel infinite.

Even as her body buzzed with fire from her mate's touch, Exie pulled away a moment later, hooking her fingers in the hem of Septima's tunic and lifting it over her head before tossing it to the side. "You shouldn't stay in wet clothes either, my flame. You'll catch a chill."

Rich brown skin shone in the candlelight, water from Septima's wet clothes leaving a sheen on her skin. Exie took her in for a moment, blown away by the beauty of her mate's body, before reaching forward to unlace Septima's trousers, letting them slide to the floor. Once her mate was bare before her, the scent of her arousal made it difficult for Exie to think about anything else. She kicked off her boots, dropping her soaking trousers to the floor.

"I don't think I can catch a chill with you, Exie." Septima's voice was no more than a purr as she crawled onto the small bed, her curvy backside in the air as she looked at Exie from over her shoulder. Exie stepped forward, climbing onto the bed beside her.

"Why is that, my flame?"

When Septima rolled over onto her back, pulling Exie on top of her, the mischievous grin on her face could have sent any male or female to their knees. "Because you're so hot, of course."

The side of Exie's lips lifted in a smile. "Is that so?"

Before Septima could respond, Exie leaned down, retaking her lips.

Their tongues met, tangling together and igniting a fierce fire within Exie's core. Their mutual desire was ready to explode like a dragon's fiery breath.

As the flames of passion raged in her heart, Exie's hands roamed, caressing the familiar curves of her mate's body. Septima's skin was warm beneath her fingers, the heat radiating from her like the sun on a summer's day. Exie shed her fear and grief, allowing herself to be consumed by the love that blazed between them.

With one hand still exploring Septima's curves, Exie trailed her other hand down her mate's body, leaving a trail of goosebumps in her wake. She traced the delicate lines of Septima's breasts, her fingers brushing over the tight peak of her nipple, causing her mate to arch her back, her hips shifting restlessly beneath her.

"You're so beautiful," Exie whispered, her voice hoarse with desire.

Kissing her way down Septima's neck, her lips found Septima's swollen peak, her teeth grazing lightly before her mouth enveloped the taut nub.

Septima's breath hitched, her fingers tangling in Exie's long hair, a gaspy moan leaving her lips. The sound made Exie smile against Septima's skin, her tongue flicking at the sensitive nipple again before she moved to the other breast, giving it the same attention.

Her lips traveled lower, her hands guiding her way as she traced a path down Septima's body, her fingers teasing the smooth skin of Septima's stomach until they brushed against the soft curls between her legs.

The sight of her mate's arousal, damp and swollen, sent a wave of desire coursing through Exie, and she couldn't hold out anymore, slipping two fingers inside Septima, feeling the heat and wetness surrounding her digits. For so long, she had wanted nothing more than pleasure from the females she'd brought to her bed, having lost someone she loved so dearly, but Septima was different—a human female still so young, decades younger than Exie. She had taken her body, heart, and soul so completely.

Septima's moans were like a siren's song, only filling Exie with more fire, with a deeper need to please her. Each slow creak of the ship matched the rhythm of her hand, drawing out exactly the response she sought from her mate. Using her mate's body language as a cue, she quickened her pace, fingers sliding in and out with a rhythm that matched the rhythm of her heart, massaging the sensitive spot inside that drove her mate wild. Septima's hips moved in time, her breath coming in short pants. Exie continued to explore, her fingers slick with Septima's arousal as she traced a path from her entrance to her clit, her touch feather-light. Septima's moans filled the small cabin, her body begging for more.

The scent of sex filled the air as Exie lowered her head between Septima's thighs, eager to please her mate. She licked her lips, savoring the taste of her mate's nectar, before diving in with abandon.

Her tongue danced over Septima's swollen folds, tracing the curves and dips.

"Oh," Septima whimpered, her hips undulating against Exie's face. "Please."

Knowing what her mate needed, Exie slipped her finger back inside, the tight heat of Septima's core clenching her fingers. Her mouth continued its work, sucking and licking the bundle of nerves at Septima's apex, the taste of her mate nearly sending her eyes back in her head.

As Septima's breaths became shorter, her moans more frantic, Exie doubled down, her fingers increasing their rhythm. Watching her mate's pleasure-addled face from under her lashes, Exie hummed softly, the vibrations causing Septima to shudder violently, her hips thrusting harder against Exie's mouth.

When the spiral burst, Septima cried out, her muscles clamping tightly around Exie's fingers, her body shaking with the force of her climax.

With one final lick, Exie pulled her fingers away, her own desire surging through her body at the taste of her mate. She slowly moved up Septima's body, their eyes locked, the passion between them like lightning.

Hand finding Exie's face, Septima's fingers brushed through Exie's wavy hair, her thumb tracing the edge of Exie's mouth.

"You are the love of my life, Exie," Septima whispered, emotion pouring through her dark eyes. "I can't imagine a world without you."

Exie smiled, love warming her chest. "And I can't imagine a world without you, my flame. You're my everything."

Wrapping her legs around Exie's waist, Septima flipped them over until she was straddling her. As Exie watched her mate's stunning body in the candlelight, Septima reached into the satchel beside the bed, taking out the flexible phallic-shaped rod they often used in their lovemaking and sliding it through her release where it still glistened between her folds. Exie couldn't turn away; every move Septima made filled her with desire even more.

Exie gasped as Septima pressed the rod inside her before lowering herself onto the other end, connecting their bodies as one. Their eyes met, and Septima's gaze deepened, keeping Exie spellbound. Her body trembled with the intensity of the connection, the desire building between them like the tempestuous sea they had just fought.

With a cry, Exie thrust her hips upward, meeting Septima's every move as their bodies melded together, both their juices slickening the object connecting them, allowing it to go deep enough to allow their bodies to touch—to rub together and increase the pleasure.

Moans growing louder, Septima's breath came in short gasps as she rode Exie. The object between them stretched Exie's tight walls, sending shockwaves of pleasure through her body with each thrust, her gasps mingling with her mate's.

Exie's fingertips dug into the soft flesh of Septima's hips, her nails leaving crescent shapes in Septima's smooth brown skin. The sight of Septima's pleasure only fueled her own desire, and she arched her back, meeting each of Septima's thrusts with equal passion. The desire coursed through her like a wildfire, igniting her body and soul.

Their bodies moved in perfect sync, the rhythm of their love-making echoing throughout the small room. The air was thick with the scent of their arousal mingling with the smell of the sea and salt in the air.

As their passion reached its peak, Exie and Septima cried out, their arms gripping each other tightly as their hips rolled through their orgasms.

In the aftermath, they lay together, gasping for breath, their bodies entwined in a tangle of limbs and sweat. Exie's gaze was locked on Septima's, her love and devotion evident in every ounce of her heart.

"I love you," Septima whispered, pressing a lingering kiss to Exie's lips. "You are my world."

Exie smiled, tracing the lines of Septima's face with her fingers. "And you're mine, my flame. Forever and always."

Outside, the sea exhaled; inside, Exie traced a slow circle over Septima's sternum, sealing a vow she would spend her life keeping.

Chapter Eighteen

Aurelia

Creaking timber and the gentle sway of the ship woke Aurelia from dreams filled with visions of phoenixes soaring over tempestuous seas. She blinked away the remnants of sleep, her eyes adjusting to the modest light that peeked through the porthole. With a stretch, she rose from her bed, the ship's rhythms now a familiar dance beneath her feet, although they still turned her stomach slightly. The lull of calm seas felt almost indecent after the violence of the storm, as though the ocean itself was catching its breath.

Cristos had already left their quarters, probably to go above deck and speak with the captain, so she pulled on her cloak and headed out in the same direction.

Upon stepping onto the deck, the warmth of the sun kissed her skin, a welcome contrast to the biting cold of the storm that had raged just the night before. The skies were a vibrant azure, and the calm sea stretched out endlessly before her, its surface shimmering like a sea of diamonds.

"Good morning, Your Majesty," called out Alteria, the healer, from across the deck where she tended to Rockie and Nikoleta, who were resting in lounging chairs in the early morning sun.

"Morning, Alteria." With a genuine smile, Aurelia made her way over to join the healer. "How are they doing this morning?"

"They're doing much better," Alteria replied, her voice warm as the gentle rays of the sun. "Their wounds are healing nicely." The scent of poultices mingled with salt and tar, the fragrance of survival carved from hardship.

Aurelia nodded, kneeling beside Rockie to inspect the warrior's bandages. "Rockie, how do you feel? Are you in any pain?"

"Better, Your Majesty," Rockie responded, wincing slightly as Aurelia adjusted her bandage.

"Please call me Aurelia, Rockie. I'm still the same person who stayed up drinking with you and Exie while you both tried to teach me how to play that game I could never figure out."

With a chuckle, Rockie nodded. "It was a fun night. We definitely need to have another night like that once we are more settled."

Nikoleta lay nearby, her eyes closed and breathing steadily as Alteria applied a fresh poultice to her bruises. Aurelia moved to her side, offering assistance where she could. As she did so, her thoughts drifted to the responsibility weighing on her young heart—the lives of those in Ekotoria and those in the human realm who depended on her success. Every bandage and every bruise she saw seemed to stitch itself into her conscience, a tally of what she owed to both the living and the dead.

With the injured warriors tended to, Aurelia stepped away, allowing them time to rest. As she made her way across the sunlit deck, the gentle sea breeze brushed against her fiery red hair, easing her troubled thoughts. A smile spread across her lips when she found Cristos, Exie, Septima, and Bremusa gathered near the ship's railing, their eyes focused on the distant horizon. A thin seam of cloud stitched the sky to the water, resembling destiny if one stared long enough.

"Only a few more days until we reach the Inferno Territories," Cristos said, reaching out for Aurelia's hand and pulling her against his chest as he pressed a gentle kiss on her lips. "Good morning, my love. How did you sleep? I didn't want to wake you."

She beamed up at him, always happy to see her handsome husband in the morning. "I slept pretty well. Is there anything we should prepare for when we arrive?"

Although she was in Cristos' arms, she directed her question to the group. Bremusa looked toward the horizon, always seeming to see what everyone else could not. "We should work on honing your new powers, my queen, as well as your ability to fly."

A numbing sensation washed over Aurelia at Bremusa's suggestion—fear, she realized—but she also understood that the fear was misplaced. Learning to use her new powers, along with her wings, was important. However, she hadn't seen her new crimson appendages since the war, and even acknowledging the power that now hummed through her veins was intimidating.

Aurelia lowered her chin. "Shall we take a walk and talk, Bremusa?"

After giving Cristos a kiss on the cheek, Aurelia stepped away from the group, following behind the female she knew held much wisdom, along with secrets about her mother that no one else knew.

The wind whispered through Aurelia's fiery red hair as she and Bremusa walked side by side along the deck, the sea stretching endlessly around them. The salty sea breeze filled her senses as she squinted against the bright morning sun. The ship rolled gently beneath her feet, a far cry from the violent tempest that had battered them the night before.

"Ever since I arrived at the Aegrician war camp, when my sister and I first ran away from home, I've had these... visions," Aurelia began, her words hesitant. "I've been able to see through Otera's eyes. I thought they were dreams at first, not knowing who Otera was or how I fit into this world. Somehow, I was able to witness what she saw when she was in the dungeon of the Aegrician palace before the war. Even in her most lonesome moments, I was somehow there with her, although I was nothing more than a specter."

Halting in her steps, Bremusa's silver eyes widened with surprise. "You've seen through Otera's eyes?" she asked, intrigue lacing her voice. "This is a rare ability, one I've only read about in ancient texts." Bremusa's gaze sharpened, not with doubt, but with the keen assessment of a strategist who had just learned of a new kind of blade.

Aurelia nodded, her mind racing. "What could it mean? And why Otera?"

Leaning over the railing, Bremusa went quiet for a moment, seemingly pondering the question. Aurelia rested her forearms on the railing beside her, watching as two dolphins swam in front of the ship. "Before you became queen, I told you that Otera needed to sacrifice herself for you to fulfill the prophecy and take her place. Although I don't know for sure, I believe there is a connection between the two of you that grants you this ability."

Even though Bremusa's words lacked concrete evidence, they made sense to Aurelia. The truth was, the recent events in their world were unprecedented, so no one had all the answers—not even Bremusa.

"You mentioned wanting to teach me how to use my powers..." Aurelia blew out a breath, glancing over her shoulder. "And my wings."

Seeming to sense her unease, Bremusa smiled. "I can't imagine how difficult it must be for you to go through so many changes in such a short amount of time. Your mother was always one to face challenges head-on, with an adventurous spirit. Gods..." Shaking her head, a smile crept up the side of her lips. "She was infinitely rebellious—never afraid to do what she wanted, even if it wasn't befitting someone of her status. It drove your great-grandmother mad. I remember the last day we spent together before she was forced to flee. We snuck out of the palace to go to the Dusty Lantern for a few drinks, leaving

Otera to entertain her grandmother's court. Otera hated it, but Messalina hated it even more. All she wanted was adventure, not the life of a royal. She would have been so proud of the woman you've become, Aurelia. I promise you that."

The mention of Messalina washed over Aurelia like sunlight glimmering on waves—both dazzling and painful—illuminating the absence that influenced her every choice. Tears pricked at the corners of her eyes, and she blinked them back, swallowing against the lump in her throat.

It was both comforting and overwhelming to learn more about the woman who had given her life—a woman she missed more than words could express, a woman whose legacy continued through her. "Thank you, Bremusa. Your guidance means more to me than you can imagine."

"Remember," Bremusa began, turning to face Aurelia fully and placing a hand on her forearm, "that I am here for you, just as I was for your mother. Together, we will face whatever challenges the Inferno Territories hold and find the missing portal. Then we will return home so you can lead your people into the future and raise your child in peace."

Aurelia gazed at the moonlit sea, its surface shimmering like a thousand tiny stars. The sea breeze ruffled her hair, bringing with it the scent of salt and some unknown floral aroma.

"Thank you," she said, turning to the dark-haired elemental beside her. "Your help means more to me than I can express."

Bremusa smiled, an unusual sight on such an intense face. "Of course, my queen. I was the one who told your mother that her future daughter would be queen, so I consider it an honor to mentor you on this journey."

For the next two days, as the ship made its way toward the Emerald Enclave on the southernmost tip of the Inferno Territories, Aurelia and Bremusa dedicated every spare moment to honing Aurelia's new powers. Although they also worked on meditation, they began by attempting to summon Aurelia's wings, which she found incredibly challenging. She hadn't seen her wings since the end of the war, but she believed they were still there.

"Remember to focus on your core," Bremusa instructed as Aurelia closed her eyes, the energy within her body swirling and shifting.

With a deep breath, Aurelia visualized her wings emerging, the same as she had been doing for the past two days. This time, however, she felt a sensation of feathers sprouting from her back. A rush of adrenaline coursed through her, and she exhaled. Suddenly, her wings burst forth—vibrant and bristling with magic. The weight pulled at her back, but the surge of freedom overshadowed the strain. Her new form was a promise written in feathers and fire. Achieving this lifted a

weight from her shoulders, just as the approval on her mentor's face did.

"Beautiful," Bremusa said, smiling as her own stunning golden wings erupted from her back in a burst of fire. "Now let's work on controlling them."

For hours, Aurelia practiced extending, retracting, and manipulating her wings under Bremusa's watchful eye. Even Cristos joined in a few times, offering a more detailed explanation of how his wings worked, although his were quite different and did not retract. There was still so much about flying that her husband could teach her. Each day brought progress but also challenges. Her muscles ached from the effort, and her mind grew weary from the strain.

On the third day, they turned their attention to Aurelia's newfound ability to create fire. She had used it during the war and to destroy the crown, but she had been unable to summon it since then.

Aurelia sat cross-legged on the quarterdeck near the stern, staring at her hands and focusing her energy on generating a small flame. The first few attempts yielded nothing more than a few sparks, but with Bremusa's guidance and persistent encouragement, Aurelia eventually managed to produce a flickering flame in the palm of her hand. Its light trembled, fragile as a newborn star, yet it carried the same gravity: potential vast enough to burn or to save. It wasn't enough to melt a crown or set fire to a pyre, but it was a start.

As the sun dipped below the horizon, its final blaze made the edge of the world appear ablaze. Aurelia closed her eyes, her breathing steady.

"Allow your mind to drift," Bremusa said, kneeling just inches in front of her on the deck. "Visualize the connection with Otera as a thread woven between you. Once you find the thread, follow it..."

Although Aurelia didn't know what she was looking for, she concentrated on Bremusa's words, reaching out for the ethereal connection she shared with her aunt. The distant sound of laughter from somewhere below deck reminded her of the others, but she pushed those thoughts aside, focusing intently on the task. However, no matter how hard she tried, she couldn't feel Otera, and all she saw was the darkness behind her eyelids. "I can't force them to come to me. Maybe she's too far away."

Shoulders slouching, Aurelia opened her eyes to find Bremusa just inches from her own. The look of disappointment on her mentor's face made her stomach sink. "It's okay to fail," Bremusa said gently. "What's not okay is giving up and never trying again. Eventually, you'll not only be able to reach into Otera's mind, but you'll also be able to connect with others, which can be a power beyond measure. However, it can also be dangerous." Bremusa's eyes held no jest; some doors, once opened, could never be shut, and Aurelia felt the weight of that warning burrow beneath her skin.

Leaning forward, Bremusa placed her slender hands on either side of Aurelia's face, her elemental power sending warmth through Aurelia's skin. "Now, envision extending that thread, branching out to others whose mental walls cannot keep you out. Perhaps one of the crew, someone who wouldn't know how to protect their mind from such an invasion."

Aurelia furrowed her brow in concentration, her heartbeat slowing as she immersed herself in meditation. She could almost feel the threads stretching, connecting her to unseen minds. The sensation was both exhilarating and frightening. It felt like progress, and as they worked over the next few hours, Aurelia found it easier to locate the thread and pull on it.

As they finished their meditation session, the tantalizing aroma of roasted vegetables and freshly baked bread wafted through the air, signaling that dinner was ready.

Opening her eyes, Aurelia blinked against the twilight and smiled at Bremusa as she stood and brushed off her tunic. "Thank you. I'll keep practicing."

Together, they joined Cristos and the rest of their group on the upper deck, settling around the rough wooden table laden with food that had been stocked when they arrived at the harbor. Outside, a shimmering fog enveloped the ship, casting an eerie glow over the wooden planks and swaying sails as it drifted closer to the Emerald Enclave. The mist swirled like a living thing, curling tendrils over the ship as if testing whether they were intruders or guests. Aurelia gazed out at the misty horizon, anticipation and trepidation battling within her.

"Tell me more about Queen Thesipha," she asked Bremusa, her voice barely audible above the gentle lapping of the waves against the ship's hull.

"As I mentioned before, Queen Thesipha is a dryad, a forest nymph with a deep connection to nature." Although they couldn't see through the haze that surrounded them, Bremusa looked ahead, her silver eyes reflecting the eerie light of the fog. "She rules over the forest spirits that dwell in her palace, which is situated within the oldest of trees. Its bark bears centuries of petitions, with each leaf rumored to remember the hands that pleaded beneath it."

"Will she be willing to help us?" Exie asked, looking up from her plate of roasted vegetables.

Bremusa nodded. "I believe so. Queen Thesipha has always been an ally to those who seek peace and harmony, but just because she believes in your cause doesn't mean she will fight for it. If we can convince her that our quest for the missing portal will prevent war from reaching her shores, she will hopefully grant us her aid."

As the moon rose, the group slowly dispersed, leaving Aurelia and Cristos alone. They wasted no time heading to their quarters, exhaustion making Aurelia's limbs feel heavy. The moment Cristos closed the door behind them, she went directly to the copper tub in the corner of the room, which was filled with steaming hot water poured by one of the ship's crew.

"Do you want some company?" Cristos asked, pulling off his boots and placing them beside the door.

Aurelia nodded, untying her tunic and draping it over the back of a chair. Over the past few weeks, her flat stomach had begun to swell—not by much, but enough to reveal that she was expecting. Cristos' eyes roamed over her figure, the cerulean blue of his gaze deepening with heat.

"I'm not sure how well we'll both fit," she said playfully.

Undeterred, Cristos smirked as he crossed the small room, sliding his arm around her waist and pulling her close. With the weight of the world on her shoulders, Aurelia sank into him, closing her eyes in relief.

"One more day, my love. One more day and we'll be off this ship, at least for a little while," he reassured her.

Nuzzling against his chest, she wrapped her arms around him and rubbed her hands up his back to the base of his wings. "Hopefully, we can find what we're looking for and return home—for good this time."

Aurelia didn't need to hear Cristos agree; she could already sense that he felt the same way. They all did.

Leaving the hope for a quick resolution hanging in the air, Cristos undressed and climbed into the copper tub behind Aurelia, his magnificent wings draping over the back. The ship wasn't nearly as comfortable as the palace, but it was certainly better than living in a tent camp—aside from the seasickness. They were fortunate to have a tub at all; there were only a few on the ship, and they had been inviting their friends to enjoy theirs since the first day. Everyone was ready for the luxury of private amenities once again.

"Can you believe we'll soon be parents?" Cristos asked, enveloping Aurelia in his strong arms and pulling her against him. The question lingered in the steam, fragrant with hope and fragile as glass.

Closing her eyes, Aurelia shook her head, a smile forming on her lips. "Sometimes it feels like a dream."

Cristos nodded and gently tapped her shoulder, signaling for her to lean forward. After so many shared baths, she knew he intended to wash her hair, and she felt grateful. Her eyes remained closed as he poured warm water over her, fingers massaging lavender soap into her hair. "Have you thought about names?" he asked.

The question made Aurelia smile wider, warmth blooming in her chest. With everything else happening, she'd spent very little time thinking about the life growing inside her, and that needed to change. "For a girl, I think I would like to name her Lina, after my mother. If it's a boy, perhaps Faidon, after the friend you lost. Unless you have another name in mind?"

Cristos shook his head, squeezing some of the water from her hair. "Both are very special names. No matter what, our child will be cherished—the most loved in all the continent." Saying the names aloud filled the quiet with hope, soft as the sunrise on still water.

With their skin still damp from the bath, Aurelia and Cristos slipped into bed, their bodies still bare. Aurelia traced her fingers along the smooth, damp skin of Cristos' chest, feeling the steady rhythm of his heartbeat beneath her touch. Their eyes locked, the fire between them burning brighter than the candles that surrounded them.

"You've been working so hard with Bremusa over the past few days," Cristos said, leaning forward to brush his lips against hers. "I'm proud of you."

The pride in his eyes told her he meant what he said. "Thank you for believing in me."

Brushing his lips across hers again, Cristos' fingertips traveled along her collarbone, down the curve of her breast, and further still to the swell of her belly where their child grew within her. His touch was gentle yet possessive, as if he sought to claim every inch of her as his own, although he already had, both inside and out.

"Your beauty takes my breath away. It has since I first laid eyes on you," he murmured against her neck, nipping at the sensitive skin there before moving lower to capture one of her nipples between his lips.

Aurelia gasped, arching into him as pleasure rippled through her body. Her hands tangled in his dark hair, urging him to keep kissing her, keep touching her. It had been days since they'd made love, and her body needed him. He kissed and sucked, the sensation sending lightning straight to her core.

"Cristos."

With no clothes between them, the hard bar of his cock slid against her entrance, teasing her with the promise of bliss if only he shifted his hips a little. "What are you asking for, my queen?"

The moment the words left his mouth, he rolled against her, his erection sliding through her juices until the tip of him breached the surface. Before he could pull back, she wrapped her legs around him, pulling him inside.

A groan rumbled out of Cristos' chest as he thrusted deep, filling her in the way she'd craved to be filled, the tension in her body melting away as he moved inside of her. If fate was to be believed, they had an entire lifetime to go slow, but this wasn't the time.

They made love hard and fast, Aurelia's whimpers undoubtedly heard across the entire ship, but she didn't care. She loved her husband, and her body sang for him, so when their climaxes washed over them, neither one of them stifled their moans.

Spent and tangled, Aurelia whispered a silent vow into Cristos' shoulder—that no matter the storm ahead, their child would know a world worth living in.

Chapter Nineteen

Aurelia

The sun rose over the awakening sea, shedding light on a sight that was almost too breathtaking to be real—a mirage—an oasis in the endless blue that would surely disappear before they could touch it. The breeze fluttered Aurelia's hair, the brine of the sea mingling with a floral scent she couldn't place. The fragrance seemed to drift from the land ahead, as if the forest was already reaching across the waves to greet or warn them.

"Land ho!" Exie called out from her precarious perch on one of the masts. Aurelia marveled at how she could hold on without falling; the phoenix warrior had proven to be capable of circus-level aerobatics. The two sisters looked up at her and snickered.

Beside Aurelia, Septima stretched and rubbed her eyes. "Finally! I've never been so ready to set foot on solid ground."

Aurelia mirrored the sentiment, but trepidation still weighed down her feet on the wooden planks below. They had no idea what awaited them in the unruly forest ahead, nor how the queen of that land would respond to their unannounced intrusion, and that filled Aurelia with unease. She instinctively brushed her hand against her stomach, feeling the weight of both crown and child pressing heavier than armor.

Squeaky hinges pierced the silent air as the crew lowered the anchor and dropped the sails, ensuring they didn't get too close to the land. Not only was there no harbor, which made it difficult to approach the coast safely, but if they needed to make a fast getaway, they wanted the ship to be able to set sail without navigating shallow waters.

"Are you ready?" Cristos asked, stepping up from behind her, his voice catching Aurelia by surprise and sending her heart leaping. She nodded, allowing him to lift her into his arms. A downward flap of his wings sent them launching into the air. Behind them, Exie and Bremusa transformed into their phoenix forms, while Septima climbed onto Exie's back. Vasilis brought up the rear of their group, but Rockie and Nikoleta were forced to stay behind with the healer, as they were still recovering from their injuries.

The lush canopy of the Emerald Enclave spread across the southern end of the continent as far as Aurelia could see from the air. The sight was magnificent, but she knew danger lurked somewhere within the shadows. The treetops moved in a single hush, as though the forest spoke a warning she had not yet learned.

Landing on the grassy coastline, Cristos set Aurelia down beside him, reaching over his shoulder to unsheathe his sword before dipping his chin to Bremusa. She was the only member of their group without a weapon in her hands. Even Aurelia notched an arrow into her bow, scanning the treeline for any movement.

"Do you think they know we're here?" Exie asked, taking a step forward to shield Septima from view. Bremusa tilted her head as if in thought, but before she could answer, a rustling came from the forest ahead. Two dryads stepped out of the brush—forest nymphs, creatures Aurelia had only ever heard of in fairy tales.

A few inches shorter than Aurelia, the two female dryads blended nearly perfectly with their environment. Aurelia rubbed her eyes to ensure she wasn't imagining them. When she reopened her eyes, the two dryads were still there. The air around them smelled of rain on leaves and crushed mint, a living signature of the grove they guarded.

Dressed in flowing robes the color of clovers, with intricate braids twisted throughout their long hair, adorned with dozens of multicolored flowers, the two ethereal creatures took hesitant steps forward. In the early morning sun, their skin shone like leaves kissed by dawn's light. Their wide eyes glinted with the wariness of deer in twilight, narrowing with distrust as they observed the newcomers.

Beside Aurelia, Bremusa reached into her satchel, making one of the nymphs jolt in surprise. The nymph's fear faded when Bremusa held out a single golden acorn. The small object caught everyone by surprise. Aurelia had never seen an acorn in such a color; it gleamed like a sun trapped in seed form, pulsing faintly as though alive.

Lifting the golden acorn before her, Bremusa dipped her chin, a gesture that silently conveyed to the dryads that she meant them no harm.

"A gift," Bremusa said, her tone soft, her eyes even softer. "A gift for your queen if she would honor us with her presence and listen to our plight. We mean no harm to your people or your land. We come in search of aid, not conquest."

After a moment of silence, the two nymphs exchanged glances, sharing an unspoken thought before they nodded in unison and turned their fixed stares back to Bremusa. Although they may not have fully trusted her or the rest of the group, they seemed at least willing to bring them to their queen.

Suddenly, the dryad on the right, whose hair was nearly as brilliant a crimson as Aurelia's, sprang forward and took the acorn from Bremusa's palm. With a gesture that seemed to summon the morning breeze, she nodded. "Follow."

At that singular command, the nymphs remained silent as they turned their backs on Aurelia and the rest of her group, darting back into the forest. Although Aurelia felt uncertain, it appeared that Bremusa understood their silence, giving a single nod to Aurelia before following the nymphs deeper into the woods.

Navigating through trees and brush, Aurelia and the others followed the two tree nymphs for what felt like hours, moving further away from the relative safety of their ship. Aurelia walked beside Cristos, their hands brushing against each other occasionally, a subtle reminder that he was there. Roots like ancient ribs rose from the earth, and the light grew dimmer, creating a quiet green hush that made their breathing sound unnaturally loud.

"Are we doing the right thing by trusting them?" she whispered to him, hoping only he could hear.

Cristos met her gaze, his blue eyes steady. He squeezed her fingers gently. "I don't think we have any other choice."

As the group continued to follow their guides, Aurelia's thoughts swirled like a tempest, grappling with the dangers that lay ahead. The forest grew denser, making the path nearly impassable. Soon, the landscape shifted, leading them away from the ground altogether.

Ascending the spiraled roots that twisted skyward, the group approached Queen Thesipha's court—a palace not built, but grown within the arboreal citadel. The living architecture of interwoven branches and blossoms resembled something out of pure fantasy. The path itself seemed to breathe, roots shifting minutely underfoot, reminding Aurelia that this was no dead stone hall but a living body of wood and leaf.

They were led through two massive double doors made from the thick branches of an oak tree into a windowless chamber guarded by two satyrs. The room was dimly lit, casting eerie shadows against the gnarled roots snaking around its walls. A chill ran down Aurelia's spine as she studied the satyrs—creatures she had only encountered in fairy tales, never imagining they were real. Although humanoid, their muscular bodies were covered in coarse fur, with tails and twisted horns sprouting from their foreheads. They leaned against their spears, their golden pupils glinting in the half-light, their feral stares unblinking, making Aurelia feel as though prey had willingly wandered into a den.

The tension in the room was palpable, tightening Aurelia's chest. Cristos' jaw became rigid, revealing that he felt the same unease. No one seemed willing to speak, especially not with the satyrs watching them as if they were plotting to take over the kingdom.

Finally, after what felt like at least an hour of waiting, another set of doors creaked open—doors Aurelia had not even noticed before. They revealed a grand walkway lined with towering trees, sparkling lights hanging from their branches. Aurelia couldn't help but gasp at the sight. Branches interwoven with vines formed a canopy high above, dappling the floor with golden sunlight. The air was thick with the scent of blooming flowers and damp earth. A hush fell from the leaves, as if the forest's attention was turning to the throne.

As they entered the throne room, Aurelia's gaze locked onto Queen Thesipha, who sat perched upon a living throne woven from the roots of a colossal tree. Her eyes were sharp as emeralds, and her expression was guarded and unreadable. Although the queen of the Emerald Enclave dryads was no taller than any of the females in their group and bore no visible weapons, Queen Thesipha radiated power. It was palpable in the air around her, as though the entire forest was holding its breath, waiting for her command. Flowers unfurled at her feet in slow motion, responding to her presence as if she were spring incarnate. Aurelia swallowed her insecurity and hung her bow back over her shoulder in a gesture of peace. They were outnumbered anyway.

The two satyrs who had watched them like hawks in the waiting room now stood by her side. A blond-haired female pixie perched on her shoulder, her tiny wings tucked tightly against her back. Aurelia forced her spine to straighten, even though she felt tired and was nowhere near confident enough to represent the fae world—a world she had only just begun to be a part of, even if it flowed through her blood.

"Speak," the queen commanded, her voice melodic but her tone stern. "Tell me why you dare intrude upon my realm."

"Your Majesty," Bremusa began, bowing from the waist. "We come seeking your aid in our quest to find a portal that has disappeared from our land—a portal my people are fated to protect, which may be hidden on this continent. The portal is missing, and one of the most powerful artifacts in our world has been stolen. We mean no offense or harm to you or your people, but if we don't find these items, we are all in danger."

"Many have sought my help only to betray me in the end," the queen replied coolly, narrowing her eyes. "Why should I trust you?"

Aurelia clenched her fists at her sides, the weight of their mission heavy on her shoulders. Taking a deep breath, she attempted to summon every ounce of courage before speaking. "Your Majesty," she began, her voice steady and strong, "my name is Aurelia Vesta, descendant of the great queen Faenia Lumino and niece of Otera Lumino, the queen of Aegricia, until she sacrificed her life to protect the portal that separates our realm from that of the humans. She sacrificed herself to fulfill the prophecy that placed me on the throne."

"Is Otera Lumino dead, then?" Queen Thesipha asked, her eyes widening.

Grief tugged at Aurelia's stomach, even though she knew her aunt was very much alive. She shook her head. "When the framework for the portal was destroyed, sending its magic to become lost in our realm, Queen Otera and many others rose from the ashes. She was dead, but she is now alive."

Curiosity flashed across the dryad queen's face as she leaned forward in her throne, but it cleared quickly. "That's impossible."

Everything Aurelia knew about the world told her that the queen was right, but Otera was dead, and she was now alive.

There was no question about that, no matter how improbable it seemed.

As Aurelia struggled to prepare an explanation that could convince the queen, Bremusa touched her arm, searching her face for permission to speak on her behalf. Aurelia nodded.

"I understand your disbelief and hesitation, but we did not come this far to deceive you. The fate of our world depends on finding this portal and keeping it out of the hands of those who would exploit it for nefarious purposes. I know you have doubts, but please understand that our intentions are pure. We aim only to locate the portal and return it to its rightful place."

The queen fell silent for a few moments, her fingers drumming against the armrests of her throne. The tension in the room made Aurelia's skin crawl as they waited for a response; each second felt like an eternity. Finally, the queen sighed and nodded, acknowledging the gravity of the situation. "Very well," she said, reluctance still evident in her voice. "You will need to stay here as my guests until at least tomorrow while I speak with my people and make arrangements. I will send two of my most powerful trackers with you, along with a few guards, to assist in your search and to protect our interests. Our land must be safeguarded at all costs; it is our lifeblood."

Bremusa dipped her chin and took a step back. For a moment, Aurelia thought the queen was dismissing them, but when she scanned their faces, it was clear the queen had more to say. Aurelia swallowed, eager to hear the queen's following words.

"Be wary, outsiders," Queen Thesipha warned, her voice regaining its edge. "My Enclave is ancient and full of secrets. Tread carefully, lest you unleash something that cannot be contained." The branches overhead rustled, though no wind stirred, as if the Enclave itself agreed with her warning.

Chapter Twenty

Kason

Kason and Holera slept in the day after their excursion into the caves off the coast of Embershell, neither of them discussing the sensation that had overcome them inside the grotto—how the magic of the the coral seemed to lure them into the water, how something after they'd left just felt *different*. After they'd come down from the high they'd given to each other when they made love, they'd made it safely back to the tavern and had gone to sleep. They were both drained, as though the cave had taken just as much as it had given.

Waking the next day, Kason's head spun as though he'd drowned in several mugs of whiskey, and it took him a moment to get his bearings and remember where he was. But beside him was the most important person in the world to him, so he got caught up in her before he thought too hard about it.

Holera rolled over onto her back, her eyes still sleepy as she looked up at him. "I haven't felt this drained after a full night of sleep in a long time, if ever."

Sliding his hand up to cup her cheek, Kason leaned forward and kissed her gently on her lips, savoring the spark he felt every time he touched her. "You must have needed sleep, my fierce warrior."

The night wrapped Embershell in its velvety embrace as Kason and Holera, shrouded in shadows, made their way back to the clandestine caves. The moon was a crescent, barely more than a silver eyelash against the dark canvas of the sky. The damp sand muffled their steps as they walked down the dark beach, Kason's eyes fixed on the yawning maw of the cavern ahead—a different cave from the one they'd found themselves in the night before.

"Look," Kason whispered, his gaze fixated on the faint lights up ahead—a boat disappearing around the curve of the continent. "Something's happening up there. They were definitely anchored somewhere up ahead."

Holera nodded, her silver hair catching the scant moonlight from beneath the hood of her cloak, every strand that was no longer dyed black. Their footsteps echoed softly off the damp walls as they entered the opening of the largest cave, Kason's hand on the hilt of his blade as he walked a step ahead of his mate.

On near-silent feet, they ventured deeper into the darkness, where the sound of the sea faded to a ghostly murmur. Faint echoes of movement reached them—the clink of metal, the muffled thud of heavy objects being set down. Intrigue quickened Kason's pulse, drawing him onward like a moth to a flame, although they were undoubtedly stepping into a potentially dangerous situation.

Rounding a corner, they found themselves in a larger cavern, illuminated by flickering torchlight dancing across the walls. At least six figures, draped in darkness, caught Kason's eyes, their silhouettes hunched over crates that seemed to swallow the light. They appeared to be organizing whatever was inside the crates, but Kason and Holera were too far away, and it was too dark to see what was inside.

"Who are they?" Holera whispered, her voice barely audible over the dripping of water from the stalactites.

Kason shook his head. "I don't know." Turning back toward the figures, his eyes narrowed, trying to make out more details in the dim light.

With one more glance at Holera, he brushed his hand against hers for a brief moment before edging closer toward the crates, keeping to the shadows. He strained his ears, attempting to catch snippets of conversation among the figures, but the air in the space shifted, the hair on the back of his neck standing on end. His instincts screamed danger, but before they could move, the sound of footsteps approached them from behind. They were trapped. *Cornered.*

"Who are you?" A gruff voice sent Kason's heart into the ground beneath his feet. He whirled around, his protectiveness over Holera surging within him. Fear gripped him like a vice, but he refused to let it show. He was by no means a weak male, and his mate was as fierce a warrior as any Aegrician warrior, but they were outnumbered.

"Speak!" another voice barked, and Kason opened his mouth to respond when suddenly a sack was thrust over his head. Panic bubbling inside him, he reached for Holera's hand, but she was quickly pulled away from him.

"Let us go!" she screamed, the desperation in her voice like a sword to his soul. "We can explain!"

A low chuckle was the only response she received.

"Please don't harm her." It took everything inside Kason to remain calm as hands pulled his arms behind his back and bound them together, the cold blade of a dagger poised at his throat. "Let her go. Just take me."

There was no response, but he could hear the rustling of them doing the same to Holera beside him.

The rough hands gripping Kason's arms sent shivers down his spine; the scent of body odor and whiskey assaulted his senses. Multiple people dragged them toward the shoreline, the sound of crashing waves growing closer with each step. The sack over his head made it difficult to breathe, as did the panic seizing his lungs.

"Where are you taking us?" Kason demanded, his voice muffled by the fabric of the sack. There was a brief silence before a gruff voice replied.

"Shut your mouth before I gag both of you."

Despite the threat, Kason leaned to the side, his shoulder brushing against hers before he was pulled away.

They walked for several minutes across the sand before the ground beneath their feet became more solid—a ramp, Kason realized. A sudden lurch beneath his feet signaled that they had been led onto a small boat, the gentle rocking making it even more challenging to maintain his balance when someone else was forcing him to move without him being able to see.

Led to the rear of the vessel, they were both forced to sit down on a wooden bench, Kason's body instinctively scooting closer to his mate the moment she dropped down beside him. Their captors' hands were no longer on them, but they weren't far away.

The journey felt like an eternity as the boat slid through the calm waters of the Elder Sea, anxiety mounting with every stroke of the oars. When the boat finally came to a halt, Kason's heart pounded in his chest, the uncertainty of where he and his mate were being taken tightening his chest.

"Get up!" one of the captors growled, yanking Kason roughly to his feet. Unable to help himself, he growled right back, but forced his temper back when Holera's fear changed her scent, turning it bitter. If something happened to him, he knew she would be left alone to fend for herself, and he couldn't let that happen.

For the length of several blocks, they were escorted side-by-side, Kason stumbling when the wooden docks met the stone ground of the mainland.

Hinges squealed as two heavy wooden doors were pulled open and they were forced inside a building and down a long hall. When they were pulled to a stop, Kason's breath stilled.

"Remove the sacks," a smooth, authoritative voice commanded, one Kason knew well. A shiver of dread ran down his spine.

When the sack was pulled off Kason's head, he blinked furiously against the sudden brightness, but when his eyes adjusted, he recognized the opulent throne room and the male sitting on the throne. At the heart of the room sat King Ailani, ruler of Diapolis, his piercing turquoise eyes fixed on Kason and Holera with a mix of curiosity and displeasure.

"Care to explain why you're spying in my capital, friends?"

Chapter Twenty-One

Aurelia

Night fell over the lush landscape of the Emerald Enclave, with the palace blending seamlessly into the surrounding nature, illuminated by the moonlight. The air was thick with tension as Aurelia and her companions gathered around a table draped in gossamer silks. Aurelia's mind was restless as she considered what lay ahead.

After meeting with the dryad queen, they had been shown to their guest rooms within the palace and treated as honored guests. If the queen still harbored doubts about their intentions, Aurelia couldn't tell. However, the queen had immediately gone to meet with her advisors upon bringing Aurelia and the others to their private chambers. The knowledge that their fate was being discussed without their input only deepened Aurelia's anxiety. Every bite of food felt like consuming borrowed time, and every glance at her companions reminded her that they were already facing judgment without a defense.

"Queen Thesipha was not making an idle threat," Bremusa observed, her silver eyes reflecting the flickering candlelight as she sipped her wine. "Having her people accompany us as we travel inland will certainly help, but there are dangers on this continent that even I cannot confront. We will have to rely on their guidance, even if it's clear they still do not trust us."

The ever-stoic Vasilis nodded, pouring more wine into his goblet. "Trust isn't easily earned, but I believe that once they get to know us better, they'll see that we are genuine. If we don't restore balance, it could also negatively impact their land. I believe the queen understands that."

Exie leaned back in her chair, stretching her long legs beneath the table. "Let's just hope her people are as powerful as she claims. I'm a damn good tracker, but I know nothing about this continent except what I've read."

Sensing the weight of their shared unease, Aurelia cleared her throat, attempting to exude the confidence that the queen had just shown. "I realize this alliance is fragile, but we must trust that the dryads will honor the queen's commitment to our cause. We cannot let doubt weaken our resolve. This is too important."

The lush canopy of the Emerald Enclave arched over them like a protective cloak, but Aurelia could not shake the weight on her shoulders as they departed from the sanctuary of the dryad palace. The air was fragrant with the scent of damp earth and wildflowers, but it did little to soothe her simmering nerves.

Cristos' shadow loomed beside her, his hand brushing against hers as a reminder that he was there for her. He always had been.

Walking alongside the two dryad trackers, Solitaria and Gillia, Bremusa's silver eyes scanned the forest, clearly following a trail that Aurelia couldn't sense. She enjoyed working with Bremusa on the ship, but since making landfall, she had found it challenging to work with the elemental again. The two dryad trackers moved with innate grace, their forms blending seamlessly with their surroundings, while the satyr guards, Joc and Strov, flanked their group, their cloven hooves treading lightly on the mossy ground, weapons at the ready. Their presence was a constant reminder that hospitality was conditional; the Enclave's eyes walked beside them in flesh and horn.

The tree canopy was too thick for them to keep track of time, but Aurelia knew hours had passed by the burning in her leg muscles and her intense desire to collapse. Still, they kept hiking, each footfall taking them deeper into the heart of the forest where sunlight merely dappled through the leaves in fleeting golden kisses upon the forest floor. Shadows pooled like ink between the roots, and Aurelia could not tell if the hush belonged to reverence or ambush. The air itself seemed to thrum to life, vibrating with the unseen current that Bremusa navigated, her connection to the land serving as their compass through this realm of towering trees and hidden dangers.

"Are you sure this is the right path?" asked Gillia, one of the dryads. They were supposed to be the group's guides, but instead, they had allowed Bremusa to take the lead—not that anyone could have stopped her.

"Trust me," Bremusa replied, not even turning to glance at the dryad who had asked the question. "My connection to the Shadow Glass will lead us to the portal. If they are together, I will find both."

"Right," said Solitaria, her voice tinged with doubt as she exchanged a glance with Gillia before falling silent.

As they moved deeper into the forest, Aurelia couldn't help but marvel at the beauty surrounding them—towering trees adorned with leaves of every hue, crystal-clear streams cutting through emerald moss. A fragrant breeze rustled the leaves, carrying the songs of birds and the distant murmur of a babbling brook. It should have been a scene of perfect serenity, but Aurelia's heart was heavy with unease.

Cristos' hand hovered near her elbow as they navigated the uneven forest floor, never straying more than a few inches away from her side. "Watch your step, my love."

Nodding, she smiled faintly and reached out to take his hand. Her eyes darted nervously between the shadows of the trees, haunted by Queen Thesipha's warnings about the dangers lurking in the enchanted realm. Despite their strong party, she couldn't shake the feeling that unseen eyes were watching their every move. After being ambushed by hellhounds and Warbotach barbarians in Spectre Forest, Aurelia was no stranger to surprise attacks. With those she loved by her side and a child growing inside her, she didn't want to take any chances.

"Are you alright, Aurelia?" Cristos asked in a low voice, ensuring he wouldn't be overheard by their companions. He rarely addressed her by her first name, so his concern was apparent. Since they had left the palace, he had been vigilant in caring for her, making sure she had enough water and food, even offering to carry her so she could rest her legs—something she had already accepted.

Running her fingers through her fiery hair, Aurelia shrugged. She knew she couldn't hide her feelings from her mate, her husband. "I'm just... uneasy. I'm not sure if it's the feeling of being watched or if it's just the power of suggestion making me believe there are eyes on me when there aren't."

He lowered his chin and wrapped his arm and wing around her, pulling her close. "Her concerns were meant to keep us alert, not to paralyze us with fear. We are well-prepared for whatever may come our way. I won't let anything happen to you or those we love."

His confidence felt like a lifeline, but Aurelia's instincts coiled tightly, whispering that love alone might not be enough to keep the shadows at bay.

As the sun sank low, casting its fading golden rays through the foliage, the group emerged from a thick grove to find themselves on the banks of a breathtaking river. The water shimmered like liquid silver, reflecting the vibrant colors of the surrounding landscape. Despite the beauty of the scene, tension prickled at the edges of Aurelia's consciousness.

"Look at this," Septima exclaimed, her awe temporarily eclipsing the worry that had plagued Aurelia all day. Turning her gaze to the water, Aurelia tried to allow the soothing sounds of its flow to relax her. Their journey had already been emotionally and physically draining, and all Aurelia really wanted was to stop and rest. However, as they approached the water's edge, a guttural growl echoed through the trees, followed by the sound of snapping branches. The silver water lost its serene shimmer; it seemed to recoil, warning them of the predator breaking through the wood.

Feeling her heart drop into her stomach, Aurelia reached for her bow, notching an arrow as the rest of her group drew their weapons. Cristos stepped in front of her, but she maneuvered to the side, aiming toward the treeline.

From the shadows of the forest, a monstrous beast lunged at them—its teeth bared and eyes filled with malice. It was a hellhound. Its fur appeared to smoke, as if fire smoldered beneath its hide, and its breath reeked of iron and rot, the stench of nightmares made flesh.

"Take cover!" Septima shouted, pulling one of the dryads behind her just as the creature swiped its massive paw, barely missing Septima's arm.

Vasilis spun around and slashed at the beast, slicing across its front leg. As it shrieked in pain, he scooped up Gillia and soared into the sky, taking her safely across the river.

"Exie, Bremusa! Get them across the river!" Cristos commanded, his wings unfurling as he reached for Aurelia.

"We can't leave them!" she protested as Cristos lifted her and launched into the air, leaving the two dryads behind. Aurelia watched, breath caught in her throat, as Exie and Bremusa shifted into their majestic phoenix forms to carry the others to safety. But the beast, furious, surged toward Septima before they could help.

"No! Exie!" Panic seized Aurelia's lungs as she watched from above—the beast snarling and snapping while the others struggled to hold it at bay. "Cristos, we have to help them! Just let me take the shot!"

Not waiting for his permission, she reached into her quiver for another arrow, aiming it at the creature, even though she knew she was too far away. She was about to scream at him, about to wiggle loose, but Cristos flew them a little closer, allowing Aurelia to get the creature in her sights.

The taller of the satyrs, Joc, jabbed his spear at the creature, black blood splattering on the ground as a hole was torn into its side. But it did not stop; it swung around, wrapping its jaws around Joc's wrist. The satyr screamed, trying to free his arm while the other satyr, Strov, provoked the creature to lure it away.

Frustration boiled through Aurelia as she tried to get a clear shot, aiming for the creature without hitting the two satyrs. They were moving too much, making it far too risky to shoot, but she had no choice. The satyr was losing too much blood, and the beast wouldn't let go. Taking a deep breath to steady her nerves, Aurelia lifted her bow, took aim, and fired. Time slowed; the string bit into her fingertips, her heartbeat syncing with the arrow as if her entire world balanced on its flight.

Chapter Twenty-Two

Variel

Raindrops clung to the edges of Variel's fur cloak, each one shimmering like a tiny crystal as they rolled off into the muddy streets. The scent of damp earth filled the air, mingling with the familiar tang of iron and wood—the lifeblood of any human settlement. The oracle wolf shifted her weight from foot to foot, trying to keep warm in her humanoid form. Something tugged at Variel's instincts like a thread caught in her claws—subtle but insistent—a nudge that the day had changed direction.

"Good day to you," she called out, her voice barely audible above the din of the rain as she approached the store owner. "I'm looking for supplies, clothing, bandages, and such."

"Ah, of course!" the man replied, his eyes darting between Variel's obsidian gaze and the pouch of gold she offered. "Right this way."

As they walked through the cluttered aisles, Variel's fingers brushed against the rough-hewn surfaces of wooden shields and cold iron blades. Each item carried its own story, the whispered memories of battles fought and lives lost. Her thoughts wandered back to her comrades in the camp. They needed supplies, and more importantly, they needed to find the portal and get back home.

A flash of fiery red hair across the market caused her heart to skip a beat, nearly sending her crashing into a rack of tunics.

"Excuse me," she said, her voice sharp, her eyes darting from the woman across the street to the human man before her. "Who is that woman?"

"Something wrong?" the store owner asked, concern creeping into his voice as he followed her gaze.

"Who is she?"

Looking from the woman with flowing red hair back to Variel, the man nodded. "Ah, that's Lina, the dressmaker. She's been in town for years now. A fine craftswoman, I must say. Keeps to herself, mostly, but she's very kind."

The moment the name Lina left his lips, Variel's heart flopped like a fish out of water in her chest, but she did her best to hide her disbelief. Names carried power, and this one struck like a key turning in an old lock.

"Thank you," she murmured, her mind still racing. The woman bore a striking resemblance to Aurelia—Cristos' Aurelia—the queen of Aegricia. Every feature of her face and every curl of her crimson hair mirrored that of the queen. It couldn't be a coincidence. The only problem was that Aurelia had no biological sisters, and Aurelia's mother, Messalina Lumino, was supposed to be dead. She had been killed by Joneira's assassins more than a decade prior. Yet, here she was, in the flesh, a radiant smile spread across her stunning face as she spoke with an elderly customer about a dress that needed mending.

"Will this be all?" The shopkeeper's voice brought Variel back to the present abruptly.

"Yes, thank you," she replied, her eyes never leaving the very-much-alive Messalina Lumino as she passed the gold coins into the man's hand. Her thoughts churned like the stormy skies above, weighing the risks and rewards of approaching this woman and wondering if she was simply imagining things. Every fiber of her being screamed that it was too dangerous to trust anyone in such uncertain times, but the lure of such a powerful ally, so closely connected to Aurelia, was too strong to resist.

The only question was: what could she possibly say to a woman who had faked her death to protect her realm and her family? How could she tell her that the foe who had once wanted her dead could be anywhere, ready to finish what she had started all those years ago? The moment Variel approached Messalina Lumino—the moment she said her name out loud—she knew she could be signing Messalina's death warrant.

A soft gust of wind tousled Variel's obsidian hair as she stood in the shadow of a towering oak, watching the red-haired dressmaker from a distance. The woman's nimble fingers expertly worked on a silky fabric draped over her arm, making her appear glamorous, with the tips of her ears appearing rounded. She seemed human, but Variel could scent the fae on her. Glamour softened the lines of her ears, but scent could not be deceived; the truth hung in the air, bright as iron. There was no doubt about which world she came from. Variel's heart raced as she steeled her nerves, trying to formulate the words to bridge the chasm between them.

Blowing out a breath and forcing a smile across her aged face, she stepped into the sunlight, approaching the dressmaker's booth. "Excuse me."

The dressmaker looked up, cerulean eyes meeting Variel's gaze. "Can I help you?"

After just one glance into the woman's eyes, Variel had no doubt about who she was in the presence of. It took her a moment to find her words and catch her breath.

"Is everything okay, ma'am?" Messalina asked again, her blue eyes softening with concern.

A hush fell over the marketplace as a sudden gust of wind whipped through the stalls, carrying with it the scent of impending rain and the promise of a storm to come. Variel scanned the area around them, ensuring no one was in earshot before she spoke.

"Please know that I come to you with the most honorable intentions," she said, reaching out to touch Messalina's hand. The moment their skin met, Variel forced a surge of her power through their connection, relief flooding her heart when Messalina's eyes widened. In that instant, Variel knew she would be believed.

"Please understand, I did not come here to seek you out, Lina. I didn't know you were alive—no one in my world knows you're alive, but you are in danger, and your daughter needs our help in our world. We need to speak in private. Soon."

Even in this moment, the wrong word could unmask a life carefully stitched together. Variel kept Messalina's true name hidden behind her teeth.

Messalina's eyes widened, shock coloring her features. "My d-daughter?" she stammered, quickly composing herself. She glanced around nervously, as if fearing that someone might be listening in on their conversation. "Meet me at dusk in the forest, beyond the eastern edge of town. There is a small cottage there, hidden amongst the trees. We can speak privately there."

The sun dipped below the horizon, casting deep shadows across the forest as Variel strode toward the eastern edge of town. Her heart pounded in her chest, echoing the rhythm of the raindrops that began to fall from the darkening sky. Every one of her lupine senses was attuned to the world around her, ensuring she wasn't being followed until the cottage came into view, at which point she shifted back into her humanoid form.

Through the windows of the small wooden structure, candlelight flickered, creating silhouettes of the figures inside. Variel hesitated for a moment, taking a deep breath before knocking.

"Variel," Messalina said, stepping aside to allow her in. "This is my husband, Proteus," she continued, resting her delicate hand on the forearm of the dark-haired man standing behind her, "and my son, Amadeus."

As Variel entered, she dipped her chin, taking in the appearances of both males. It only took her a moment to notice how much Amadeus resembled Aurelia. However, his hair was a dark brown like his father's. "Nice to meet you both," she said.

Messalina allowed her husband to wrap his arm around her waist. "Do you bring news of our daughter? Of our daughters?"

"Indeed." The gravity of the situation tightened Variel's chest, forcing her to swallow. "Aurelia and Septima are in our realm—Ekotoria. Dozens of warriors and I are trapped here, searching for a way back. The last time I saw Aurelia was during the Battle of Flamecliff. Messalina... Joneira is trapped here with me."

Proteus's stance had the economy of a seasoned soldier; Amadeus's gaze flashed a protective heat, quick as flint. Amadeus's eyes widened in shock as Messalina's hand flew to her mouth, tears welling in her eyes. Proteus's hands clenched into fists at his sides.

"Tell us more," Messalina urged, her voice trembling with emotion.

Variel took a deep breath, but her gaze turned toward the decanter of whiskey on the counter. "Shall we sit and have a drink then? This may require something strong."

The whiskey rose warm as a hearth, passing a small measure of courage hand to hand.

Once they were all seated in the small area in front of the fire, mugs of whiskey in hand, Variel took a deep sip, savoring the burn on the way down before daring to discuss something so dire. "A war rages in the fae realm," she began, her voice growing steadier as she recounted the unfolding events within Ekotoria. "Warbotach invaded Norithae and then Aegricia before attempting to overtake the entire continent." She blew out a breath, locking eyes with each of her listeners, who hung on her every word. "At first, we didn't realize there was anyone behind Warbotach's invasions, not until the War of Flamecliff, when Joneira invaded Aegricia with dragon-wielding armies from the Inferno Territories. During that conflict, the portal controlled by the Aegrician crown was destroyed, its magic dispersed, and we—and Joneira—were dropped into the human realm with no obvious way to return home."

"Joneira?" Proteus growled, his anger a palpable force within the cramped space. "What does she want? What role does she play in this?"

Taking another sip of her whiskey, Variel turned her eyes to the fire. "Her motivations are unclear, but we know she poses an imminent threat to all we hold dear." When she looked back at those sitting across from her, she made eye contact with each family member in turn. "We cannot afford to underestimate her."

If Joneira found a foothold here, she would not only finish old work—she would plant the seeds for new wars.

"Then what do you propose?" Proteus asked, his voice calm despite the storm raging both outside the cottage and inside his deep blue eyes.

Variel did not need to ponder her answer. "We must unite. We must gather our allies and face Joneira head-on, for the sake of our families, our people, and our realm."

"At first light, we move," Proteus declared. "No rumors left behind, no names spoken in the open."

The mountains loomed like slumbering giants, their silhouettes etched against the starlit sky. The air was cool, and Variel's breath created wispy clouds in front of her as she walked. Owls punctuated the darkness with low calls, while the underbrush seemed to hold its breath, as if even the smallest creatures knew to remain silent. With their decisions made, Variel and her companions left the cottage under the cover of darkness. They headed toward the camp they had set up further up the mountain.

Messalina had spent years in Breqan, building a life there, but nothing was more important to her than returning to her homeland to reunite with her daughters. After Variel shared her truth about the war and what had brought her to the human realm, Messalina recounted her struggles to keep her family safe. She detailed how her husband had helped her fake her own death and hide her away in another land, allowing the threat against her to diminish. Until that point, Messalina and her family had lived under constant threat, facing several assassination attempts from Joneira against Messalina and even her children. Removing herself from her home was the only option that Messalina believed she had, and it seemed to have been the right choice. Under the protection of their father and the care of servants, Aurelia had grown into a wonderful young woman.

From what Variel learned during their dinner together, Messalina's husband, Proteus, had left his position with the Vaekrosaean government after Aurelia and Septima ran away. He and Amadeus had traveled to Breqan to reunite with Messalina, and they had been together ever since. Before that, Proteus had only seen his wife while on military campaigns; it was where they had first lived as a married couple. However, Messalina had not seen her son since she left home, disguised as a dead woman. Variel could see the depth of Messalina's love and longing for her children in her eyes. She had lost so much of her life and family because of Joneira, and now that Joneira was back, Variel wondered who would want to kill whom more.

As they hiked higher up the mountain, the forest grew denser, casting shadows that melded together into an impenetrable wall. With three more souls beside her—two humans—the weight of the darkness pressed down on Variel like a leaden cloak. She palmed a charm at her belt, anchoring a quiet ward behind them so their trail would fade like mist. She knew their enemies could be lurking anywhere, and bringing Messalina into her group only heightened the risk. Yet there was no turning back, nor would Messalina have wanted to. Now that Messalina knew her daughters were in Ekotoria and needed her help, nothing could have prevented her from finding a way back to them.

"Stay close," Variel murmured, her voice barely audible over the rustling leaves. "The path is treacherous, and the night holds more than shadows."

Messalina nodded silently, determination etched on her features like armor. Even in the dim moonlight, her eyes sparkled with a fire kindled by years of hiding, now burning with the need to act and fight for the future of her bloodline. Proteus, steady beside her, surveyed the forest with the practiced gaze of a trained soldier, his officer's wisdom providing unspoken comfort. Amadeus appeared as a fierce protector, ready to spring into battle to safeguard his sisters.

They ascended higher, where the chill bit deeper and the stars seemed to draw closer, curious observers of their clandestine journey.

As they approached the camp, apprehension coursed through Variel's veins; she was uncertain how her people would respond to Messalina's reappearance. With a gesture, she parted the veil of their protective wards, stepping into the secure perimeter of the camp, with Messalina and her family following closely behind. The air cooled upon her skin, and a familiar pressure eased as the camp's quiet magic accepted them.

Variel caught Thalius' scent before she saw him. The Norithaean warrior stood guard not far from the camp's perimeter. The slide of his sword and the rustle of his wings told her he was aware of their approach.

"Stand down, Thalius," she called softly enough for him to hear. "It's just me."

For a moment, everything fell silent; only the sound of their gentle footsteps against the leaf-littered ground broke the stillness. But as they stepped into the clearing, a deep gasp shattered the quiet.

"It can't be," gasped Kalliopi Icarus, an Aegrician warrior standing beside Thalius, her mouth agape and golden eyes wide. "Messalina?"

The name rippled through the clearing—shock followed by a dawning relief that felt like rain after a drought.

Variel's gaze shifted from the fiery-haired princess at her side to the dark-haired warrior, then back again. By the time she turned her eyes back to Messalina, the princess was already running, throwing her arms around Kalliopi. It was clear in that moment that Messalina would be received with open arms by her people, no matter how long she had been gone. Around them, lanterns brightened one by one, as if the camp itself had decided to welcome her home.

CHAPTER TWENTY-THREE

Aurelia

The fading sun created deep shadows between the ancient trees of the Emerald Enclave's wild forest as Aurelia's group gathered around the injured satyr. His breathing was labored, and blood oozed from a deep gash in his arm where the beast's teeth had dug in. The bite had ragged edges where the teeth had torn through skin; heat throbbed under Aurelia's palm, even through the cloth. Aurelia's heart clenched with worry as she watched Bremusa cover the wound with her hands, a silver glow emanating from her pale skin. Although Bremusa wasn't a healer, she possessed healing abilities among her many powers.

"Will he be alright?" Aurelia asked, stepping closer to Cristos, who pulled her even closer to him. Even though she knew it wasn't her fault they were in this situation, she couldn't shake the feeling of responsibility for the satyr's injury. That thought felt like iron—useless guilt, yet stubborn as blood.

Bremusa didn't look away from her patient. "His injury is severe, but there is deep magic in this land and magic in his blood. My powers can do the rest, but we must set up camp here tonight so he can rest."

Cristos nodded, his strong arms wrapping protectively around Aurelia. "We'll set up camp. Take all the time you need."

For the next hour, wards were created around the small camp as tents were erected and a fire was lit. The wards settled with a soft pressure in the air, a hush that felt like a hand over the camp's mouth. The queen had graciously provided them with food for their journey, so the dryads prepared a meal of root stew. The injured satyr was set up inside a tent beside his comrade, resting peacefully under a concoction harvested from the surrounding forest that aided in pain relief.

"Tell us more about the Emerald Enclave," Septima prompted, stirring the stew with a wooden spoon as it hung over the fire. "What dangers lie ahead?"

Solitaria sighed, her green eyes gazing into the distance, where the forest was illuminated by thousands of luminescent bugs. It was breathtaking, and Aurelia could tell that the dryad agreed, even though she had lived there her entire life. "This land is filled with enchantments and ancient magic. It's wondrous."

"You must be careful, however," Gillia chimed in. "Creatures roam these forests—dangerous ones like the hellhound that attacked us, and the terrain itself can change without warning to protect itself. It's a beautiful place, but it is not safe. Don't let its beauty fool you."

"Paths have been known to fold back on themselves, and clearings can vanish like a breath on glass."

As the fire's embers crackled and glowed, Aurelia snuggled into Cristos' side, watching the flames. Bremusa approached her. "May I speak with you privately?" she asked, her silver eyes gleaming in the moonlight.

After a brief glance at Cristos, Aurelia nodded. "Of course."

She gave her husband a quick kiss on the lips and followed Bremusa toward the edge of the campsite, where a gentle stream babbled. The grass soaked her ankles, and the stream's breeze carried the faint scents of resin and crushed mint, a clean contrast to the campfire's smoke. Aurelia looked across the water, where fire sprites had just begun their nightly dance among the foliage. "What's on your mind, Bremusa?" she asked.

Bremusa lifted her hand, a spiral of silver light swirling at her fingertips. "Earlier tonight, I was thinking about whether you and I can combine our powers to locate the portal," she began, her voice hushed. "I believe we might amplify each other's abilities. Our connection could be strong enough for us to sense the portal's presence or for your visions to reveal its location."

"But we must be careful," Aurelia replied. "Shared sight can blur the self. If I pull too hard, I could drag you deeper than you intend."

After days of working together on the ship, the idea didn't surprise Aurelia. Still, she also lacked confidence in her ability to summon useful visions. Still, for her people, she would try anything. So, although she was unsure, not that she could have been sure of anything, she sat down on the grass-covered ground beside Bremusa and reached out her hands. "Let us try."

Beneath the shadowy canopy of an ancient oak tree, Aurelia and Bremusa intertwined their fingers, palms pressing against one another as their eyes fell closed. The energy between them pulsed and hummed like the gentle rhythm of a heartbeat, causing Aurelia's own heart to slow. Her hearing narrowed; each heartbeat became a distant drum in fog, and soon the camp, the fire, and even Cristos faded to the far side of a pane of glass. She didn't think about anything in particular, simply allowing the surge of power from her friend's hands to fill her, while the bubbling of the stream soothed her.

For what seemed like hours, but was probably only minutes, their bodies swayed gently in unison, as if drawn together by an unseen force. Time lost all meaning, and the world around them faded until only their shared consciousness remained.

Suddenly, Aurelia gasped as a surge of energy unlike anything she had ever experienced coursed through her veins. She gripped Bremusa's hands tighter, trembling with the force of the energy within her.

"Something's happening," she whispered, her voice barely audible. "Can you feel it?"

As if a door had opened, allowing a flood of power to wash over them, darkness enveloped Aurelia before she could hear Bremusa's response.

Aurelia's body went limp, her consciousness slipping from the physical world and plunging her into a dreamlike state. She could no longer sense Bremusa's presence or hear the gentle trickle of the stream nearby. Instead, she found herself adrift in an ethereal realm that existed parallel to the one she had been in, guided by a faint yet persistent pull that beckoned her forward, leading her through the forest by a golden thread.

A shimmering golden thread glowed before her, brightening as she wrapped her fingers around it. It hummed a note she felt more than heard—one she recognized from Otera's steady courage and her mother's voice in memory. She followed its winding path, the silken strand urging her onward through the lush landscape that shifted and blurred with every step. Whispers of a phantom wind rustled the leaves above, but they didn't flutter her hair.

"Where are you leading me?" she wondered aloud, her voice barely more than a breath, mingling with the sounds of nature. There was no response, only the unyielding pull of the thread that tugged her onward.

Fear and anticipation warred within Aurelia's chest, sending her heart pounding and her breath loud enough for her to hear. The realm felt both real and foreign, as if it were a product of her own memories twisted by some unseen force. It was overwhelming—*otherworldly*—and she was utterly alone.

Days seemed to pass as the landscape changed from dense forests to expansive plains. The golden thread never wavered in its course, even as the ethereal sun rose and set and then rose again. Aurelia's feet grew sore, her muscles ached from the constant trek, but she didn't feel hungry or thirsty, so she pressed on, driven by something innate within herself and the draw of the luminous golden string.

When day turned to night on the second day, mountains appeared before her, a deep cave nestled within, its jagged peaks piercing the sky.

"Is this where you want me to go?" Her voice trembled as she twisted the golden strand in her fingers, the entrance beckoning her where the strand disappeared within. A sense of foreboding settled in her stomach. She felt that if she entered the cave, she might never step back out. The air cooled and thinned, as if the mountain had lungs and was holding its breath. No one responded to her question, only the steady tug guiding her into the darkness.

With a deep breath and a quick glance around her, she stepped inside the cavern, the golden thread illuminating her path. Usually, she would have been scared, but at that moment, in a world that didn't quite feel real, she wasn't afraid—not in the sense that she would turn and run away. There was nowhere to run, not if she wanted to return to Cristos and Septima. If she were asleep, she would wake once the vision had finished with her. Until then, she needed to follow Bremusa's instructions and pay attention to what the vision was trying to show her.

As she ventured deeper into the main corridor, she noticed droplets of water trailing down the stone walls. An ethereal light began to pulse in the distance, casting an eerie glow across the cave's interior. The closer she got to the source of the light, the harder her heart beat, the racing of her pulse making her feel lightheaded, but she didn't stop walking. She couldn't.

It wasn't until she arrived at the back of the cave that she saw the figure standing before her and the object that person was guarding. There, in front of a swirling vortex of energy inside a large mirror with an intricately carved frame—a portal—stood a fae female. Her hair was as white as fresh snow and cascaded down to her hips. Symbols ran along the frame like ivy—some familiar from temple mosaics and others older than any script she'd ever seen. Though the female's face was stunningly beautiful, Aurelia sensed something was amiss—a hidden truth lay just beneath the surface. As she peered closer, the illusion fell away, revealing the woman's true visage, or rather the face the woman wanted her to see: a terrifying old crone, with pale eyes swirling with power that were fixed on the portal before her. The wrinkles of her face were deep against her sharp cheekbones. The shift wasn't a blink, but rather a peel, as beauty sloughed off like wet paint, revealing the bone-honest face beneath.

A gasp escaped Aurelia's mouth without her permission, and she instinctively took a step back, reaching for the dagger at her thigh. "Who are you? What is this place?"

Although Aurelia could see the female standing no more than a few feet away, the female did not respond, her attention focused solely on the pulsating energy before her. It was then that Aurelia realized the gravity of her discovery—the reason the vision had brought her to that very cave, where a portal's power resided, guarded by a being whose intentions remained a mystery. Aurelia didn't know where she was or how to get back, but she understood why she was there. The crone before her had somehow trapped the portal there, although she didn't know how or why.

Invisible and ghostly, Aurelia hovered over the crone's shoulder. Her heart raced, and her stomach turned as she gazed upon the swirling glass of the powerful mirror—the Shadow Glass. This was the object that had foretold her birth more than two decades earlier. The very thought sent a twinge of pain straight into Aurelia's soul, making her wonder how, or if, she could find her way back to the human realm through that portal and reunite with her father and brother, since her mother was gone. She missed her mother every day—a loss she would never overcome, no matter how many years passed. The energy emanating from the mirror's surface was unlike anything she had ever encountered—a storm of raw power that seemed to call to her very soul. Yet it was not just the portal's energy that held her transfixed. There was something about the Shadow Glass itself, a dark allure that drew her closer, like a moth to a flame.

"Is this all I've been searching for?" Aurelia whispered, her words lost in the maelstrom of magic surrounding her. Deep down, she knew this was the key to everything: the salvation of her kingdom, her beloved family, and perhaps even herself. Even as she moved closer, studying the crone with a cautious eye and pondering the ancient sorceress's role in the grand tapestry of fate, the crone did not react. Her eyes remained swirling, as though her body was present but her spirit was somewhere else—just as Aurelia found herself in her own plane. The thought sent a shiver through her body as she wondered if, back at the bank of the stream, her own body—her eyes—looked the same.

It was then that the unthinkable happened. After countless minutes—or perhaps hours—Aurelia had lost count. The crone seemed to sense Aurelia's presence in the room. The golden thread twanged in her fist—heard but not seen—like a warning shot through her nerves. Coming out of her trance, the crone's pale eyes snapped into focus, narrowing as they scanned the cave before finally locking onto Aurelia's ethereal form, still shimmering beside the golden thread. Blood turned to ice as fear rooted Aurelia's feet to the spot, as though her boots were made of lead.

"Who dares intrude upon my sanctuary?" the crone snarled, her voice bone-chilling and filled with rage. "I know you're here. Show yourself!" Before Aurelia could react, the sorceress raised her arms. She cast a spell that made Aurelia's spectral body flicker and waver, sending a shudder through her very being.

"Wait!" Aurelia cried out, desperation clawing at her throat. "I didn't mean to intrude. I...I need your help." She didn't know what else to say. For the first time in her vision, she was genuinely terrified. Although Otera had sensed her presence before, she had never been seen while in a vision. This time was different; her circumstances suddenly felt very serious and very dangerous.

"Help?" The crone sneered, her eyes alight with malicious amusement. It took Aurelia a moment to realize that the crone could hear her, which made her heart race. She glanced down at her hand, which was wrapped around her dagger. Her fingers were no longer spectral but transitioning before her eyes to flesh and blood. A flutter low in her belly answered the change—a protective ache that sharpened her focus. Nausea twisted in her stomach, and her thoughts automatically drifted to the child in her womb as bile crawled up her throat. "You seek help from one such as me? Foolish child, you know not what you ask."

Swallowing hard, Aurelia fought to maintain her composure, not wanting to reveal the fear that paralyzed her. "*Please*. My kingdom is in danger, and I believe the power within this glass can save us."

The crone's gaze drifted back to the swirling vortex of energy within the Shadow Glass, her hand pulling out a jagged dagger from her cloak. Aurelia froze, realizing the crone was blocking her path to the exit, and her form was nearly solid. "The portal's power calls to you, does it not? It sings a siren's song that few can resist." With her eyes never leaving Aurelia's, she took a step forward. "But beware, young queen, for its power is not easily wielded or controlled."

Taking one last look at the Shadow Glass, Aurelia bolted, skirting along the side of the cavern. The crone's blade skimmed the side of her cloak as she brushed past.

Faster than she should have been able to run, the crone chased after her, throwing a bolt of energy that crumbled part of the wall. The shock rolled through the stone; grit rained from the ceiling, and the golden thread snapped taut, yanking at her toward the mouth of the tunnel. Aurelia's spectral form flickered and wavered as she attempted to escape the crone's magic, her heart pounding like a thousand drums in her ears, matching the rhythm of their footfalls. The cavern seemed to close in around her, the air itself feeling menacing.

Cristos' voice, edged with panic, pierced through the haze of Aurelia's subconscious mind, or perhaps it was part of her dream. His words vibrated along an unseen thread, as if he had found it in her and was pulling her home.

"Come back to me, love," he pleaded. The mantra became louder and more desperate with each repetition. "Please, Aurelia. Come back to me."

Although she knew the way out of the cave, the corridor seemed to stretch longer as she ran, the end always just out of reach. The weight of the crone's presence bore down on her, threatening to trap her within the nightmare forever.

"Aurelia, please. Please. Please, come back." Cristos' cry tore through the chaos, becoming a lifeline for Aurelia to cling to. It felt as though she could sense him touching her skin, a surge of electricity affirming that he was her mate. She focused on his voice with all her might, willing herself to wake up and escape.

Stumbling over a rock, Aurelia fell to the ground, her dagger clattering as it skittered away.

For a moment, time stood still. Her body was unable to move as the crone closed the distance between them and swung her blade. Aurelia screamed and scrambled away, but just as the gust of wind from the crone's movement rustled her hair, her eyes snapped open to find herself lying on the ground, shivering uncontrollably, with strong arms wrapped around her, holding her upper body in Cristos' lap. His blue eyes were wide with concern as he pulled her against his chest.

"Thank the gods you're awake," he said, tucking her head beneath his chin. "I was so worried."

Taking a few deep breaths, Aurelia tried to shake off the lingering terror from her encounter and to understand what had made this dream feel so much more real than all the others. Though her body was drained and there was still much she didn't understand, one thing became clear as a newfound certainty settled over her mind like the first rays of sunlight piercing through a stormy sky.

"I know where it is." Her voice trembled, but the certainty within her had weight; it settled in her bones like a compass pointing true. Cristos' voice, edged with panic, pierced through the haze of Aurelia's subconscious mind, or perhaps it was part of her dream. His words vibrated along an unseen thread, as if he had found it in her and was pulling her home.

"Come back to me, love," he pleaded. The mantra became louder and more desperate with each repetition. "Please, Aurelia. Come back to me."

Although she knew the way out of the cave, the corridor seemed to stretch longer as she ran, the end always just out of reach. The weight of the crone's presence bore down on her, threatening to trap her within the nightmare forever.

"Aurelia, please. Please. Please, come back." Cristos' cry tore through the chaos, becoming a lifeline for Aurelia to cling to. It felt as though she could sense him touching her skin, a surge of electricity affirming that he was her mate. She focused on his voice with all her might, willing herself to wake up and escape.

Stumbling over a rock, Aurelia fell to the ground, her dagger clattering as it skittered away.

For a moment, time stood still. Her body was unable to move as the crone closed the distance between them and swung her blade. Aurelia screamed and scrambled away, but just as the gust of wind from the crone's movement rustled her hair, her eyes snapped open to find herself lying on the ground, shivering uncontrollably, with strong arms wrapped around her, holding her upper body in Cristos' lap. His blue eyes were wide with concern as he pulled her against his chest.

"Thank the gods you're awake," he said, tucking her head beneath his chin. "I was so worried."

Taking a few deep breaths, Aurelia tried to shake off the lingering terror from her encounter and to understand what had made this dream feel so much more real than all the others. Though her body was drained and there was still much she didn't understand, one thing became clear as a newfound certainty settled over her mind like the first rays of sunlight piercing through a stormy sky.

"I know where it is." Her voice trembled, but the certainty within her had weight; it settled in her bones like a compass pointing true.

Chapter Twenty-Four

Kason

For the first time since their arrival in Embershell, trepidation flooded through Kason. He had never been the kind of man to become easily frightened, but having his mate kneeling on the floor in front of King Ailani was not a safe situation. The air was thick with tension, nearly suffocating him, even though the sack had been removed from his head. He fought to maintain his composure. Beside him, Holera was silent, and her scent indicated that she was just as uneasy as he was. The magnificent marble floors and gold-encrusted walls seemed to mock their current predicament. The glittering chamber, intended to awe guests, only deepened his unease—beauty draped over suspicion like a mask that threatened to crack at any moment.

"Your Majesty," Kason managed, his voice strained from the pain in his shoulders caused by being tightly bound. "We came to Diapolis on a diplomatic mission. We meant no harm. You've known us for years. My mate and I are not spies."

King Ailani narrowed his eyes at the couple before him, leaning forward in his gilded throne, his finger tracing the carvings on the armrest. His consort, Makoa, stood by his side, as stoic as ever. "And yet, here you kneel, accused of spying in my kingdom. Do you take me for a fool?"

"Of course not, Your Majesty," Holera replied, drawing the king's turquoise eyes to her. "We have always been friendly with you and your kingdom, as has our former queen, Otera, and our new queen, Aurelia. Our sole purpose in Diapolis was to gather information that could benefit us all."

"Information?" King Ailani scoffed, his voice dripping with skepticism. "Or secrets to use against us?"

Turning to glance at Holera, Kason's chest tightened. "King Ailani, our past visits as your guests should prove our allegiance. We have fought alongside your soldiers and shared in your victories. We would never betray you or your people."

"Then explain your presence in areas of Diapolis where outsiders are forbidden," the king demanded, his tone icy and unyielding.

Hesitating for a moment, Kason exchanged a worried glance with Holera. He knew their intentions were just, and neither of them had realized the caves were forbidden. However, convincing King Ailani of that fact was proving more difficult than he had anticipated. The king of Diapolis had always been an isolationist, so forming an alliance with another kingdom was never something he seemed comfortable with. Kason straightened his spine. "After the ashes settled and friends and enemies alike departed our lands, a powerful artifact, held in our kingdom for centuries, was found to have been stolen. We don't know who took it, but we do know that if it falls into the wrong hands..." He shook his head and blew out a breath. "If this artifact, which can control the portal between worlds and can tell prophecies that can build or break kingdoms, ended up in the wrong hands, it could destroy us all. We hoped to discover the truth and bring it to your attention so we might stand united against any danger. This is far bigger than just the north or south of the continent. This affects us all."

His voice wavered despite his resolve—the plea not only for their lives but also for the fragile hope that even an isolationist king might set aside caution for the sake of their shared realm.

A flicker of something akin to fear passed across the king's eyes, but it quickly vanished. When he turned his gaze back to Kason, however, there was more kindness in his eyes than before. "Words are easily spoken, Kason. Actions speak much louder."

Taking a deep breath, Kason dipped his chin and then glanced back at his mate before looking at the king once more. "Allow us this chance to act on behalf of our shared interests, and you will see that our loyalty is unwavering. We need to work together against this threat."

King Ailani's gaze lingered on Kason and Holera, his eyes flicking between them as if he were searching for any sign of deception. After a slow heartbeat, Makoa placed his hand on the king's shoulder, a silent exchange between them that clearly carried significance. "Very well," the king finally said, his tone still more clipped than Kason would have liked. "I will grant you this opportunity to prove your allegiance. But be warned, should I discover that your loyalty has wavered, there will be no mercy."

Relief washed over Kason, easing not only his chest but also his shoulders and back as the guard unfastened his bonds. He stood behind Holera, stretching his arms before reaching for her hand. "Thank you, Your Majesty. We will not disappoint you."

The king nodded once, his long, golden curls spilling over the embroidered lapel of his sapphire jacket. "Rise and go freshen up." Behind them, the double doors of the throne room opened as two guards stepped into the entrance. "I will meet with my scouts and advisors to discuss this matter. We shall reconvene once you have had time to rest."

As Kason and Holera entered the guest room in the west wing of the palace, which overlooked the sea, he let out a breath and shut the door behind them. They both sighed, the stress of their capture and audience with King Ailani slowly dissipating now that they were alone.

"I think we convinced him," Holera murmured, a grin tugging at the side of her full lips. "But I'm still not sure if we're safe here."

Kason nodded and pulled her against his chest, kissing her deeply. "I know, fierce warrior. For now, let us take advantage of this moment of respite. I'm sure you're ready for a bath."

Her smile growing wider, Holera nodded, running her hands over her disheveled platinum hair that had become messy beneath the sack. "I'm always ready for a bath."

A large copper bathtub stood in the corner of the bathing room, steam rising from the hot water within. The Diapolisian palace was luxurious, a stark contrast to the tavern they'd been staying at for the past few days. Approaching it, Kason discarded his clothes as he went, his cock already hard from having his arms around his mate. Holera followed suit, stripping her dark clothes off and dropping them to the floor.

Holera stepped into the tub, a sigh escaping her lips. For a moment, all Kason could do was watch her. Her beauty took his breath away.

The warm water lapped at Kason's skin, soothing his aching muscles as he slid into the tub behind Holera. Taking a bath together was one of their rituals—one they both seemed to enjoy. If they could both fit in a tub, then they almost always used that time to relax together.

"I wasn't sure we were going to make it out of today," he admitted, cupping his hands and filling them with water to wet Holera's hair. Her eyes fell closed. "If something had happened to you—"

Violet eyes opened to meet his, her hand reaching for his wrist. "Don't. Don't do that. Nothing happened, and we are both okay."

He knew she was right, and he hated dwelling on the what-ifs, but seeing her bound beside him was a sight that would haunt his dreams. Still, he smiled and nodded. "I know, but I'm taking you home after this. Back to our cottage."

The words steadied him, a lifeline he clung to amid the storm of politics and war. That promise of hearth and family was the only future that mattered.

And he meant it. He was going to take her home and raise a family.

Lifting herself up in the tub, Holera spun around and slid her leg over him. "I already told you that I'm ready for that, too. I'm ready to make you a father."

The feel of her warmth enveloping him as she straddled him and took him deep sent his eyes rolling back in his head. Candlelight flickered from the sconces on the wall, casting a reflection in her dark eyes. His lips met hers in a hungry kiss the moment she was fully seated. With his arms around her, he lifted his hips to meet the roll of hers, every deep stroke stoking the fire inside his core. He marveled at the feel of her skin beneath his hands, so soft and yet so powerful.

"Maybe we can start now," he whispered, his voice gravelly with lust. He leaned in, capturing her lips with his, his tongue slipping in to taste her. Every swipe of her tongue against his spun the spiral low in his stomach tighter, until holding back his climax was nearly impossible.

Holera's head tilted back when her orgasm hit, her cunt squeezing him so tight it made his eyes water. Bracing his hands on her hips, he drove up into her harder, swallowing every moan against his lips until his own release barreled through him, leaving him breathless and more in love than he had ever been.

Yet even as bliss warmed his veins, a shadow lingered in the back of his mind—peace was fleeting, and every stolen moment with her might be their last.

Dressed in the garments provided by servants earlier that day, Kason and Holera entered the grand dining hall, where King Ailani and his consort awaited them. The tension in the room loomed like a storm cloud over the table, creating a stark contrast to the brilliant morning sun streaming through the stained glass windows. As they approached the ornate table laden with mouthwatering dishes, the king's piercing turquoise gaze remained fixed on them.

The air felt charged, as if the very light from the stained glass was struggling to reach them, bending under the weight of grim tidings.

"Please, sit," King Ailani said, his tone light despite his serious expression. Kason could sense that something was troubling the monarch, and it created a pit in his stomach. He realized that something had changed overnight, and they were about to learn what that was.

"Good morning, Your Highness." Kason pulled out a chair for Holera and then took a seat directly across from King Ailani. A servant followed closely behind, pouring hot water into their mugs of tea. "Have you found out anything new?"

King Ailani leaned forward, tapping his fingers on the table. "I met with my scouts and advisors last night. They discovered information about an elemental sorceress in the Inferno Territories. Rumors suggest she is incredibly powerful—capable of feats that belong in legends. It's said that she wishes to access the portal to create a rift between the worlds, allowing the fae to enter the realm of humans and even opening the rift that separates the veil, which would allow the dead to roam free."

The thought of an entire world bent and broken under unnatural rule made Kason's skin prickle, as if the sorceress's influence already extended across the sea.

As he processed the king's words, a cold knot formed in Kason's stomach where the pit had once been. The stakes had just risen, and the weight of responsibility bore down on him. He reached beneath the table and took Holera's hand, feeling her palm grow clammy.

"Do they have any idea where she is?" Kason asked. The Inferno Territories were a massive continent across the Irriboia Sea, along with the surrounding islands. He had only visited a few times on diplomatic missions.

Genuine concern creased the king's brow. "She's elusive, but my advisors believe she is moving north with an ancient force capable of bending nature itself to her will. If she succeeds, she could reshape our world in her twisted image, plunging us into darkness. A group of my most powerful trackers and magic wielders left for the continent aboard dragon-escorted ships this morning."

Kason exchanged a brief glance with Holera, trepidation evident in her violet eyes. They both knew their friends, and the new queen had already departed for the Inferno Territories.

If something happened to those people, it was a frightening possibility that left him struggling to breathe.

"We must return to Aegricia at once and warn our people."

Chapter Twenty-Five

Variel

The morning rays of the sun shone over the forest in the human territory of Breqan, cutting through the mist that clung to the trees like a lover's embrace. Variel stood at the edge of the camp, her keen eyes scanning the terrain ahead as she contemplated the steep ascent toward the caves where she had encountered Joneira's warriors before. The morning mist clung stubbornly to the treetops, veiling the path like a warning, as if the forest itself wished to hide what lay above. There was so much at stake if she was going to lead her people into the viper's den without knowing whether the portal was even there. Still, they dismantled their makeshift camp because they couldn't return home if they didn't search for the portal.

After she had arrived back at camp the night before with the long-lost Aegrician princess, Messalina Lumino, along with Proteus and Amadeus, the entire group sat around the fire for hours. Everyone was shocked to see Messalina and had a million questions for her about how she had managed to hide away for so long. By the time Variel curled up in her corner of one of the tents, she was exhausted.

"Variel," Messalina said, checking the straps on her bow and quiver. "We're ready to go."

With a slight nod of her lupine head, Variel set off along the trail, more than a dozen of her people following behind. The wind whispered through the trees overhead, and the scent of damp earth filled her nostrils. Moss and lichen clung to the rocks beneath her feet. She could hear the quiet conversations of the others behind her, but she didn't focus on them. Even without listening, she could feel their nerves pressing against her own—each heartbeat quick, each step too loud for a group hoping to remain unseen. Instead, she paid attention to the sounds of the forest around them. If an enemy were to happen upon them, her heightened senses would serve as their first line of defense. Despite the uncertainty in the air, Variel pressed onward.

As they climbed higher, the temperature dropped, sending shivers through Variel's fur. Icy tendrils of mist curled around her legs, obscuring the path and making each step more treacherous than the last—especially for the others. She glanced back at them, relieved to see determination still etched on their faces despite the biting cold.

After hours of hiking northward toward the place she had been just days earlier, Variel shifted back into her humanoid form and pointed to a clearing they had reached in the forest, not far from the river. "We can set up camp here."

Even as she spoke and they began to erect tents and set up wards around the campsite, a sense of threat lingered in the shadows of the darkening woods, something lurking just beyond their reach. They were within an hour's walk from the caves, and it was close enough for the power within them to call to her.

As night fell and the moon illuminated the world below, Variel shifted back into her wolf form, her senses instantly sharpening. Leaving the protection of the campsite, she led Messalina, Proteus, Amadeus, and several other warriors toward the caves, her muzzle to the ground as she searched for any trace of their enemies.

The group moved silently through the darkness, each step weighed down by the burden of their mission. Variel's ears flipped back and forth, straining to catch the faintest whisper of sound. Her nostrils flared as she caught a whiff of something—a male scent with hints of embers and freshly roasted meat. She closed her eyes, summoning the power that flowed just beneath her skin. The rest of her friends stood behind her, remaining hidden by the thick brush as she forced her power away from her body, and the wards around the enemy camp fell away. The flicker of a bonfire and approximately ten enemy warriors came into view, their laughter and conversation telling her they didn't sense the threat.

A low snarl rumbled through her chest, her lips lifting to reveal a maw filled with deadly pointed teeth. Her group moved around her, Messalina pulling her sword from its sheath. Every guard sitting around the fire looked up as her obsidian wolf form stepped out of the shadows, leaping forward with a fierce growl.

The sound of clanging steel and screaming filled the silent mountain air as Joneira's soldiers jumped up from their seats, drew their weapons, and attacked.

Messalina roared, her sword slicing through the air as it found its mark, tearing a gash into a male's ribcage. Blood immediately covered his white tunic, and he crumpled to the ground—not dead, but there was a very good chance the wound would prove to be fatal. The copper tang thickened in the air, iron and smoke mingling until every breath tasted of death itself. Although Variel's group outnumbered their enemies, several members of both sides had already sustained injuries, making them evenly matched.

Variel's teeth sank into the arm of an enemy who came after her with a dagger. She reveled in the taste of blood, but her satisfaction was short-lived. While one male struggled against her bite, more desperate to get her unattached than to get his sword that lay on the ground only feet away, another enemy blade slashed for her. Searing pain raced up her foreleg when a short sword slashed across the limb. Her vision spotted at the edges, a howl clawing at her throat. Still, she bit it back, refusing to give her enemies the satisfaction of hearing her scream.

Releasing the enemy's arm, she yelped and launched herself into the air on her hind legs, tearing his throat out before turning on the warrior who attacked her. The moment both enemies lay at her feet, she stumbled toward the treeline, her breath growing ragged. Her form shifted without her permission, but it gave her the fingers she needed to rip off part of her enemy's cloak and wrap it around her arm to stop the bleeding.

"Variel!" Messalina cried, concern lacing her voice as she dispatched another foe.

"I'm okay. Look for Joneira!" With a wince, she pulled herself back to her feet. The pain was intense, but she refused to let it hinder her.

"Amadeus, behind you!" Proteus darted toward his son, his warning arriving just in time for Amadeus to deflect the dagger aimed at his heart. Though he managed to avoid a fatal blow, the weapon grazed his shoulder, leaving a bloody gash in its wake.

"Thanks," Amadeus grunted, his face twisted in pain as he turned to fight another enemy who had pinned one of the Aegrician warriors to the ground.

As the last of the enemy warriors fell, Variel searched for Messalina and found her rummaging through the tents. The shadows swallowed them whole as they slipped between the clusters of erected structures, keeping them out of sight if any enemies lay in wait. The scent of sweat and blood hung heavily in the air, mingling with the aroma of pine. Despite her injured arm, she kept her focus sharp, her senses attuned to every whisper and rustle around them.

"Can you sense her?" Messalina asked quietly, her eyes darting from side to side, her grip tight on her sword.

Lifting her nose to the air, Variel breathed in deeply. The scent of the exiled queen was undeniably nearby. "Her presence is here, but it's faint. She can't be far."

They stepped through the forest on near-silent feet, leaving the camp behind. It didn't take long for them to realize where Joneira's scent was leading them: to the cave.

The dark granite surrounding the cave's entrance reflected the moonlight like a beacon, guiding them to what they were searching for. A cold air seeped from within, carrying the metallic scent of blood and the ancient whisper of power gone awry. Variel stopped and turned to look at the Aegrician princess beside her. Even in the moonlight, Messalina resembled her daughter so closely that, given the slow aging of the fae, she appeared more like Aurelia's sister than her mother.

"She's inside. The portal is as well—or at least I believe it is. The power is somehow warped or not in its full form, so I don't think it can be used to cross back to our world in its current state."

Worry flashed across Messalina's eyes as she undoubtedly thought of her daughters, who were still in the fae realm fighting their own battles. However, she nodded firmly. "We end this now. Once she's dead, we can figure out how to get back across. I will find a way to reunite my family."

With her dominant arm still burning in pain, Variel held her dagger in her other hand, knowing she wouldn't be able to wield it as effectively as she needed to. The two women stepped into the dark maw of the cave, their footsteps light but their breathing heavy.

"You," a female voice hissed. A flicker of fire in a palm illuminated the face of Messalina and Variel's mortal enemy. "You were supposed to be dead."

Messalina scoffed and took a step forward. "I guess you're not as good as you thought."

The laugh that escaped Joneira was pure malice as she circled Messalina, her eyes flicking to Variel. "And you... couldn't just mind your own business."

Her voice echoed like a hiss through the stone, sharp enough to cut, her eyes glinting with the fire of someone who had waited decades for vengeance.

Variel snarled, but before she could strike Joneira with her shortsword, a figure stepped out of the darkness. His face was scarred, and his eye was covered with a patch. Variel's heart sank the moment she recognized him. A walking dead man. "Uldon."

The Warbotach monarch smirked, his scarred lip lifting. "As an oracle, should you not have known I'd made it across on the back of an Aegrician before the portal crumbled?"

When the portal was destroyed, Variel had been engaged in battle with Joneira and hadn't seen what had happened to the Warbotach barbarians who invaded the northern part of the continent. She had seen them departing in ships and on the backs of hostage Aegrician warriors, so she had assumed they all perished in the blast.

Swallowing back her fear, knowing Uldon was brutal and she was injured, Variel raised her sword. His smile widened—he could undoubtedly scent her blood in the air. "It seems the rest of your warriors are gone, so you're not as scary as you used to be."

His grin fell as a snarl ripped from him. A moment later, he lunged. When Uldon swiped low with his sword, Variel met the strike, the force of it rattling her bones. Behind them, the other two women charged at one another.

"Your family will never be safe," Joneira taunted as she lunged, narrowly missing Messalina's side. "I'll hunt them down, just like I hunted you."

"Never!" Messalina roared, but Variel was too focused on fending off Uldon's strikes to assist her. Gritting her teeth, Variel caught Uldon's blade with her own and pushed back with all her strength, barely making him stumble. Her heart pounded with every strike as she charged forward again, her sword arcing toward Uldon's throat, but he quickly parried, countering with a blow aimed at her ribs.

Despite the stinging pain that burned through her injured arm, Variel managed to twist away, narrowly avoiding his lethal blade. Her breath came in ragged gasps, but her thoughts remained focused. Survival depended on it.

On the other side of the cavern, Joneira pressed forward with a flurry of blows that forced Messalina to retreat. She stumbled, her foot catching on a loose stone and sending her sprawling to the ground.

"Pathetic," he sneered, the slash of his sword barely missing her waist.

The sound of approaching boots sent hope rushing through Variel's chest. She kicked out, catching him off guard and knocking his sword to the floor. With a primal scream, Messalina rolled to the side, narrowly avoiding Joneira's blade. She then launched herself upward, her own sword finding its mark as it slid between Joneira's ribs and pierced her heart.

The others arrived from behind, with Proteus swiping at Uldon, momentarily diverting the barbarian king's attention from Variel. She fell to her knees, her chest pumping rapidly with exertion.

Only feet away, Joneira's eyes widened in shock, disbelief etched across her features as blood stained her lips. She tried to speak, but only a gurgle emerged along with the blood trickling from the corner of her mouth before she crumpled to the ground. Dead.

For a moment, Messalina stood over Joneira's lifeless body, a mixture of emotions clouding her stunning face. "This is for my mother and grandmother," she said, slashing her sword down and slicing across Joneira's neck. The exiled queen's head rolled forward, her lifeless golden eyes staring up at the ceiling.

Amid the sound of her own blood rushing in her ears, Variel heard the moment Uldon's large body hit the ground, but she didn't turn away from Messalina and the greatest enemy their kingdom had ever known. It was finally over. All they had to do was find a way back home. Yet even in victory, silence pressed down heavily; the cavern was thick with smoke and blood, and the knowledge that endings always give rise to new beginnings—some darker than the last.

CHAPTER TWENTY-SIX

AURELIA

After Aurelia had been saved from her vision, Cristos carried her into their tent, and she fell asleep in his arms. For the rest of the night, she slept soundly, free from thoughts of the crone invading her dreams.

The next morning, before she awoke, Vasilis had left with the injured satyr, Joc, taking him back to the palace. With two fewer people in their party, the group set off north toward the kingdom of Cineris, where the Voiceless Mountains cut across the center of the continent. Once they were within an hour's walk of the mountains' base, they set up camp for the night.

Later that night, with Cristos' arm draped over her waist, Aurelia's eyes fluttered open, revealing a sliver of moonlight filtering through the canvas of the tent. She lay on her side, listening to the whispers of the wind through the trees. The whispers gave way to a louder sound—or perhaps it wasn't a sound at all, but a deeper calling that burrowed into her mind, guiding her thoughts—what to hear, what to do. It beckoned her to follow. This soundless summons coiled through her mind like smoke, invasive and impossible to dispel.

Taking a deep breath, she slipped out from beneath Cristos' embrace. With the moonlight illuminating little within the tent, she did her best to find her weapons and then quietly stepped outside.

The fear gripping her heart threatened to consume her, but she steeled herself against it, or at least attempted to. Silently, she tiptoed past her friends' tents, hoping none of them would notice her absence. A pang of guilt pierced her heart, but she shook her head to clear her thoughts as she lit a torch from the fire and stepped beyond the camp's protective barrier.

"Forgive me," she whispered to everyone, her voice barely audible over the sounds of nighttime creatures. "I cannot risk your safety any longer. This burden is mine to bear." She hated the lie in those words, but if Cristos woke and followed her, he could get hurt because of her recklessness, and she could not let that happen.

Aurelia shivered as the chill of the mountainous forest landscape enveloped her; the shadows of the trees seemed to reach out and ensnare her as she moved through the underbrush. Even without the golden thread as her guide, the pull of the portal grew stronger with each step. Her heart pounded in her chest like the beat of a tribal drum, urging her forward as she approached the mouth of the cave where she believed the portal was hidden.

A cacophony of dripping stalactites and the distant rumble of an underground river filled the cave as Aurelia inched her way deeper into the darkness. The pull of the portal intensified, nearly dragging her forward as if she were being pulled by chains. She couldn't turn around; she couldn't break free. The darkness pressed closer with every step, thick as tar, as though the cave itself resented her trespass.

Suddenly, a gust of wind extinguished her torch, plunging her into complete darkness. Aurelia's breath caught in her throat, and her stomach sank as dread washed over her. Then, as if materializing from the shadows, the silver-haired elemental sorceress appeared before her. This time, she wore the face of a young woman, not that of an old crone.

"Ah, the little queen has finally arrived," the sorceress sneered, her eyes glinting like ice. "Did you truly think you could steal what I've worked so hard to find without consequence?"

"The portal doesn't belong to you," Aurelia shot back, discreetly pulling one of the daggers from her thigh sheath. "You stole it from my kingdom, where it's been for centuries."

"Such naivety." Before Aurelia could react, the sorceress raised her hand and launched a barrage of magical energy toward her. Instinctively, Aurelia dove out of the way, narrowly avoiding the deadly strike. A second later, she was running.

"Run all you want, little queen," Cyrena called after her. "But know that I will find you in the end. I'll put an end to the decades-long prophecy myself."

As Aurelia sprinted through the cave, shards of rock rained down around her, illustrating just how powerful the sorceress was. She knew she had to find a way to stop her, but she didn't know how.

When her foot caught on a jutting rock, she stumbled, losing her grip on the dagger just as she had in her vision. The dread in her stomach only grew. The dagger skittered across the uneven floor, disappearing into the shadows. Panic surged as she reached for another dagger, aware it wouldn't be effective against the elemental's power.

"Ah, there you are." With a snarl, Aurelia's attacker threw another magical strike at her. This time, it was aimed at her abdomen.

The pain that followed was like nothing she had ever experienced, a searing agony that threatened to consume her entirely. Fear rose in her chest, but something fiercer rose with it. She was more than a target; she was a mother defending a future.

"Your unborn child will never see the light of day," the sorceress hissed, her voice devoid of any trace of humanity. "And neither will you."

Clutching her stomach, tears streamed down Aurelia's face as she struggled to remain standing. She knew she couldn't give in—not just for her own sake, but for the life growing inside her. If she didn't find a way to stop the sorceress, everyone she loved would be in danger.

"Enough!" A powerful voice echoed through the cave, shattering the silence. Aurelia turned her head to see Bremusa stepping into the corridor, her silver eyes swirling with raw power. "You will not harm her, Cyrena... Sister." The revelation cleaved the air sharper than any blade, fracturing Aurelia's understanding of both allies and enemies.

The words hit Aurelia's stomach like stones, and the air suddenly felt thinner. She never even knew Bremusa had a sister.

Cyrena's icy laugh rang out, sending chills down Aurelia's spine. "So, you've finally come out of hiding, dear sister. How amusing. I thought you'd perished alongside our pathetic family."

Bremusa tightened her lips into a thin line and locked her jaw, a tendril of silver power swirling in her palm. "And you were supposed to be dead—killed for your crimes against our people. I survived your massacre, and I won't allow you to hurt Aurelia or her child. You may have faked your death before, dear sister, but you will die today."

As Aurelia cradled her arms around her middle to protect her unborn child, Bremusa launched herself at Cyrena. Their magical powers clashed in a dazzling display of light and shadows, both women vying for dominance. Silver energy clashed against ice, one power steady as a river's current, while the other was jagged like shards of a breaking glacier.

Although Aurelia wanted to help, she didn't know how. She was unsure if her power was strong enough to be of any use in the fight, but she felt it was her duty to protect the baby inside her womb, so she kept her distance.

The cave trembled under the force of their magic, rocks crashing down around them. Despite Bremusa's valiant efforts and extensive elemental powers, it quickly became evident that Cyrena was stronger than her sister.

"Is that all you've got, sister?" Cyrena taunted, her voice dripping with venom as she circled Bremusa. "You always were the weaker one—"

A sudden strike from Bremusa cut off Cyrena's taunts, but the sorceress only laughed harder, her wicked glee echoing throughout the cave.

Desperation clawed at Aurelia's insides as she watched Bremusa falter, exhaustion etched on her stunning face. She knew that if Cyrena won, it would mean certain death for both of them, for her child, and for countless others. Yet, she didn't know how to intervene without endangering her unborn child.

"Aurelia!" Cristos shouted, his wings tucking tightly against his back as he and the others surged into the cavern, racing toward them with their weapons ready.

"Too late for that." With a flick of her wrist, Cyrena directed a surge of dark magic toward the entrance, aiming at Aurelia's friends and family. Boulders tumbled down, sealing them away from one another and trapping Aurelia and Bremusa inside with their enemy.

"No!" Aurelia cried out, panic threatening to send her to her knees as she saw her friends disappear behind the rockslide. She turned swiftly to Bremusa, urgency flooding her blue eyes. "We have to do something!"

Bremusa nodded, her silver eyes unblinking. "The portal and the Shadow Glass... It's our only chance."

Together, they rushed forward, clasping their hands tightly as the hum of power from the portal flowed through them. The sensation was intoxicating yet frightening—raw energy coursing through Aurelia's veins, threatening to consume her if not harnessed correctly.

"Focus," Bremusa urged, her voice barely audible above the chaos. "Channel the power of the portal. We can do this."

As Cyrena snarled at them from only a few feet away, Bremusa threw out her arm, trapping Cyrena in an invisible web of magical energy. The sorceress's eyes widened as she struggled against her restraints, her hands held above her head.

"Your love for your people makes you weak!" Cyrena spat, attempting to break their concentration.

Aurelia did her best to focus, trying to ignore the venomous words coming from the sorceress's mouth. The light from the portal danced across Aurelia's face, reflecting in her eyes as she and Bremusa stood their ground. Cyrena's twisted visage was chilling, but Aurelia pushed those feelings aside.

"Your defiance will be your end!" Cyrena shouted, pulling one arm free. She hurled another barrage of dark energy at them, barely missing as Bremusa yanked Aurelia out of the way.

The air crackled with energy as their two forces collided—the dark energy pouring off of Cyrena and the glowing silver energy that coiled around Aurelia and Bremusa's joined hands, forming a protective shield against Cyrena's attacks. It created a symphony of destruction that echoed through the cavern, sending rocks tumbling to the ground around them.

"Impossible!" Cyrena snarled, her rage palpable. "You cannot defeat me!"

As she continued to struggle against her invisible binds, Cyrena managed to free her other arm. She thrust it forward, attempting to push the two of them back, but their shield of silver energy held firm. Aurelia had so much she wanted to say in response, but she couldn't afford to break her concentration.

As they maintained their grip on Cyrena, the portal behind her began to shift and change. Its once shimmering surface transformed into a solid black vortex.

A sense of dread trickled down Aurelia's spine, twisting her chest into a knot. "Is that—"

Aurelia's words were cut off by a scream from Cyrena, her eyes widening as she fought to escape.

Taking a step closer to her sister, Bremusa tightened her grip on Aurelia's hand. "The veil—a realm where the dead sleep in eternal slumber." Its pull felt wrong, like a tide that recedes forever without returning.

A shudder ran down Aurelia's spine at the thought of what lay behind the portal. She didn't understand why such a place would open in the Shadow Glass, but it was clear that Cyrena had stolen both for her own horrific purposes. Now, with the veil opening behind her and Cyrena at someone else's mercy, terror gripped her.

The cavern trembled, dust and debris raining down as Aurelia and Bremusa strained against Cyrena's overwhelming power. Even though Cyrena was held in place by their invisible web, her arms were free, allowing her to counterattack.

"When I count to three," Bremusa said, lifting their joined hands to raise their shield of power. Behind Cyrena, the portal roared, spinning like an oppressive vortex and whipping their hair around their faces. "We're going to push forward—give it everything we have. We're going to force her into the veil, where she should have been all along."

Gritting her teeth and wiping sweat from her brow with her free hand, Aurelia nodded.

With a shared glance, they poured every ounce of their strength into a final push. As if propelled by an unseen force, Cyrena was flung back through the air, her screams swallowed by the dark maw of the portal.

"No!" she shrieked, clawing at the air in a futile attempt to escape her fate. But the pull of the veil was too strong, and Cyrena vanished into the darkness with one last, desperate wail. For a heartbeat, the cave seemed to exhale. Yet, Aurelia knew the silence did not promise safety—only the next storm waiting to rise.

Heart pounding in her chest, Aurelia collapsed to her knees, gasping for breath. In the back of the chamber, the portal began to calm, its once terrifying presence reduced to a quiet hum.

"Is...is it over?" she whispered, her eyes fixed on the spot where Cyrena had been consumed by the veil.

Bremusa lowered herself to the ground beside Aurelia, her delicate hand reaching out to smooth across Aurelia's stomach, closing her eyes as if reading the fetus's thoughts. "Time will tell, but we have won this battle. We all have."

The sun dipped low in the sky, creating a golden crown over the horizon as the group approached the capital city of the Emerald Enclave. Aurelia could feel the gratitude from the dryads surrounding them, their presence a gentle brush against her senses. Queen Thesipha, the dryad queen, stood tall and regal, her golden hair rustling softly in the breeze.

"Your courage and strength have preserved our home," Queen Thesipha said, her voice akin to the wind through the trees. "We are forever in your debt."

With a genuine smile, Aurelia inclined her head respectfully. "Thank you, Thesipha, but we couldn't have succeeded without your help."

"Still, you've shown us the importance of unity and trust," Thesipha continued, her emerald eyes shimmering in the sunlight. "In truth, we should have been more welcoming to you when you first arrived."

Reaching out, Aurelia placed her hand on Thesipha's arm. "It's never too late to learn from our shared experiences and grow, my friend."

Thesipha nodded, her gaze full of gratitude. Even the tiny pixie on her shoulder grinned, her iridescent wings fluttering. "Farewell, Aurelia, Queen of Aegricia. Give my best to your aunt, and may our paths cross again under happier circumstances."

Aurelia wished she could believe that happiness awaited just beyond the horizon, but she had already learned how fragile peace could be.

Turning her gaze from Aurelia to Bremusa, Thesipha inclined her chin. "And to you, Elemental of Spectre Forest, Bremusa, thank you for healing Joc. His mate and children need him."

Bremusa bowed from the waist. "May the forest continue to thrive and flourish."

As they bid farewell to the dryads, the sound of waves crashing against the shore caught Aurelia's attention. The ship that would carry them back to Ekotoria awaited them, its sails flapping in the wind.

With no other work in the Inferno Territories, they boarded the craft, giving the Shadow Glass to Bremusa so she could ward it below deck. Once the Shadow Glass had gone silent, she and Aurelia locked the portal within its intricate frame, intending to return it to its home in Aegricia.

Standing on the bow as the ship began to pull away from the shore, Aurelia gazed out at the Emerald Enclave, its verdant canopy fading in the distance. The forest had taught her many lessons, but perhaps the most important was this: trust in those who stood beside her, for their strength was her strength. Together, they could rise again. Yet behind them, the forest's shadows lingered like watchful eyes, a reminder that no victory came without something left behind.

Chapter Twenty-Seven

Aurelia

The Aegrician sun dipped low in the sky, casting long shadows across the palace courtyard as Aurelia and her companions returned home from their multi-week trip to the Inferno Territories. The air was thick with the scent of pine and snow, a sweet reminder of their victory, even as much of the city lay in ruins—some parts even worse than when they had left.

As they approached the back doors of the palace, familiar faces gathered to greet them, bringing a smile to Aurelia's lips. Yet, despite her smile, she and Cristos could not ignore the twisted wreckage and debris littering the harbor and coastal areas of Embershell. Something had happened while they were gone—something significant. The harbor's broken ribs jutted from the surf, and every splintered beam felt like a warning that victory would never come without a cost.

"Kason! Holera!" Exie cried, rushing into the arms of her friends, with Septima at her heels. Relief filled Aurelia's chest as she smiled at the couple as well. Her chosen family deserved the reunion, but after two weeks away, her best friend needed her more. Even though she was exhausted and hungry, she wanted to see Kano. So, with Cristos' hand in hers, they walked across the grounds toward the massive enclosure that provided a safe home for her pet tiger.

Upon reaching the enclosure, they found Kano pacing restlessly, his muscles rippling beneath his striped fur. He looked up as they approached, his eyes brightening with recognition. In an instant, he was on his hind legs, holding onto the top of the gate. Just seeing his excitement filled Aurelia with warmth, but also guilt for having left him behind. Back in Vaekros, they had always been together, but ever since arriving in Ekotoria, various upheavals had forced her to leave him where it was safe.

"Hey there, big boy!" Reaching into her tunic, she pulled out the medallion she wore around her neck and placed it against the gate, causing the enclosure to open with its magic. By the time she stepped through the gate, Kano was already at her feet, nuzzling his large striped head against her trousers until she sat down on the ground. His golden eyes locked onto hers, expressing what his voice could not.

"I missed you, too, Kano," she whispered into his soft fur, tears pricking at the back of her eyes. His purr rumbled through her palms, easing the ache behind her ribs, if only for a moment.

Closing the gate, Cristos lowered himself to the ground beside them, and Kano automatically rolled onto his back, exposing his belly in a clear invitation for them to rub it. And they did. For the next thirty minutes—perhaps an hour—Cristos and Aurelia stayed right there, showering affection on the massive cat, who was very much a part of their family.

Once the moon was high in the sky and Kano had been given his meal for the night, Cristos and Aurelia walked back to the palace, feeling famished, exhausted, and in need of a bath.

"Ah, there you are!" Otera called out as they entered the dining hall, her fiery hair catching the light of the flickering candles.

The room was already filled with laughter and conversation, the air charged with relief at their reunion, though everyone knew there was much to discuss. Still, Aurelia couldn't help but smile at the sight of her closest friends gathered around the table: Kason, Holera, Breusa, Taryn, Otera, Blaedia, Septima, Exie, and several other high-ranking warriors and advisors, including a handsome Norithaean warrior named Lars, who sat beside Taryn, whispering in her ear as she smiled. Rockie and Nikoleta had healed nicely from their injuries before setting sail, but they, along with Vasilis and Alteria, had returned home to their families upon arriving back in the capital, so they were not seated at the table with the others. Laughter filled the hall, but a tightness lingered in the air, as if the stone itself remembered the waters that had risen where they should not have.

"Welcome back," Kason said, his boyish grin a comforting sight as they took their seats between Septima and Otera. "We only arrived back a few days ago from Diapolis."

Seated on the other side of Otera, Blaedia tilted her chin in greeting to her new queen and king, her expression serious. "Tell us everything." Aurelia interlaced her fingers with Cristos' under the table, bracing for truths that would not spare them.

"Let us not dwell on our recent hardships," Otera said, setting her whiskey glass on the table. "Instead, let's discuss what has transpired while we were apart so we can make decisions for our future."

Taryn leaned forward, pushing a loose strand of dark hair behind her ear. "An earthquake shook the city, quickly followed by a tsunami that tore through the harbor." Her eyes flicked toward the window, where the dark outlines of ruined structures could barely be seen in the moonlight. "Many buildings near the water were destroyed, but thankfully, the palace and most of our citizens were spared due to the evacuation efforts before and just after the war." Her words settled heavily in the silence, more suffocating than any stone, even as the fire crackled in the hearth.

Blaedia nodded. "There's still much damage to repair, but we've already begun the process. Our people are strong and resilient. We will rebuild, as we always have."

Beside Taryn, Lars took a sip of his whiskey, the plate of roasted meat and vegetables already empty before him. "And the Norithae camp is here to stay for as long as Aegricia needs us. If our king and queen see fit, we can send for more able-bodied citizens to come north and extend the camp. Our own seaside capital was spared."

Some of the tension in Cristos' jaw eased with Lars' words, his chin dipping in acknowledgment. Both Aegrica and Norithae had been under siege by Warbotach for months, and Cristos' own father had been murdered by the barbarians. Therefore, any good news was long overdue. Although Aurelia and Cristos were now married and ruled both kingdoms, there was no guarantee that their people would blend seamlessly or work together. Seeing that they were willing to do so, at least thus far, filled her with gratitude. It was reassuring to know that, even in her absence, her friends and family—her people—had been working tirelessly to protect and support their portion of the continent. Not that she ever doubted Otera's leadership. "Thank you all for everything you've done while we were gone," she said.

Cristos squeezed her hand and raised his glass. "Our people couldn't have asked for better guardians while we were away. A toast to all of you."

For a moment, glasses were raised in cheers, candlelight reflecting in the golden liquid in most of their glasses—most, that is, apart from Aurelia and Holera, a coincidence Aurelia had not missed.

As they sat around the table, Aurelia's heart clenched at the thought of the destruction her people had faced during her absence, but knowing most of the city had been evacuated just before the war gave her some relief. For the next hour, over dessert and tea, the group discussed their next steps, specifically how they would protect the Shadow Glass and the portal within it from falling into the wrong hands again. As the others spoke, Aurelia's eyes continued to glance out through the massive dining room windows at the remnants of the destroyed harbor, which loomed in the distance under the light of the full moon. Every time it caught her eye, it sent a shiver through her, a haunting reminder of the devastation nature had wrought upon Aegricia.

Although an earthquake and tsunami were natural occurrences, Bremusa had agreed with Otera's assessment that the release of the portal's power had caused the catastrophic event. Therefore, the sooner they returned the portal to the land, the less likely it was—hopefully—for such an event to happen again. Preventing the realm's land from unleashing punishment on them for destroying the portal had to be their top priority, even if they weren't sure it would work. Doubt had teeth, but delay had claws. They chose the path that bled the least.

The wind howled through the jagged peaks of the northern Aegrician mountains as Bremusa, Cristos, Aurelia, Septima, Exie, Otera, and Blaedia made their way along the treacherous path leading to the hidden caves after dinner. Leaning back against Cristos' chest as the horse walked forward, Aurelia pulled her hood tighter around her face to protect it from the biting cold. Due to the wind, they could not fly into the mountains as they had planned, as flying would have made the trip more hazardous.

"Are you sure this is the right place?" Exie shouted from the back of the horse in front of them, with Septima riding by her side. "All these caves look the same."

"Absolutely," Bremusa replied, her silver eyes scanning their surroundings. She didn't even have to think about it. "These caves have been protected by our ancestors for generations, and I've been coming here since before you were born. With the strength of the magic here, there is no place more secure under wards." Wind threaded through the rocks like a low voice, and Aurelia couldn't shake the feeling that the mountain listened back.

Aurelia tightened her grip on the pommel, feeling Cristos' arms tighten around her as they ascended another incline. Worry churned in her thoughts, not just for the Shadow Glass and the portal but also for her people and their kingdom. She understood the weight of responsibility resting on her shoulders, yet she couldn't shake the undercurrent of fear that she might fail if someone stole the Shadow Glass again, luring the portal away and causing the land to rebel against them.

As the group finally reached the entrance to the cave system that Bremusa had pointed out, Exie and Blaedia lit torches, the flames casting flickering shadows across the rock walls as they passed them to Septima and Aurelia. Cristos, Exie, and Blaedia lifted the Shadow Glass between them once the horse-drawn cart could no longer navigate the rocky terrain. The atmosphere grew tense as they ventured deeper into the darkness, with narrow passageways echoing their footsteps and the whispered conversations of those around them.

"Once we're inside the chamber and reinforce its wards, we'll transfer the portal's power to the new Aegrician crown. With the power that Aurelia and I summoned in the Voiceless Mountains, combined with that of Blaedia, Otera, and Exie, we should be able to create an impenetrable barrier around the cave," Bremusa said, her voice low as she took the lead. "The crown will be placed within a hidden cavity in the chamber, while a duplicate will remain in the palace for Aurelia to wear as she sees fit. With any luck, this will ensure its protection and deter any future attempts to steal it. If Uldon couldn't tell that the crown he had was a fake, then no one should be able to tell."

"Are you ready for this, love?" Otera asked, walking at Aurelia's side and searching her niece's blue eyes for any hint of doubt.

Aurelia hesitated for a moment, her heart pounding against her ribcage. The fear that threatened to consume her was just that—fear. The truth was, she wasn't alone, and that was what she needed to focus on. Pushing her hesitation aside, she nodded. "Yes. I'm ready."

As they entered the warded chamber, a wave of overwhelming energy washed over Aurelia—a powerful force that seemed to hum with ancient magic. After they leaned the massive mirror against the wall, she reached out to touch its gilded frame, her hand trembling noticeably.

"Let's do this together," Otera said, extending her hand to grasp Aurelia's. One by one, the others joined in, their hands forming a circle around the artifact and the crown. A tremor of energy gathered where their hands met, steady as a heartbeat and bright as drawn steel.

Bremusa dipped her head, closing her eyes as if grounding herself. When she reopened them, the atmosphere in the chamber shifted. "When I close my eyes at the end of the chant, you should do the same. When you feel the power shift inside you and we reopen our eyes, it will be done."

The air around them crackled with energy as the five females joined hands, their fingers intertwining tightly. The power they summoned pulsed through Aurelia's veins like a raging river, flowing from her right hand, which was held by Otera, to her left hand, held by Bremusa. Just like in the Voiceless Mountains, Aurelia didn't fully understand how to harness the magic within her veins and bend it to her will, but with her and the others serving as an energy source, Bremusa's silver eyes opened and focused on the objects before them.

"By the ancient bond that ties us, we channel this power into the heart of Aegricia," she said, her voice unwavering. A sudden gust of wind swept through the chamber, lifting Aurelia's hair and causing the torches to flicker wildly. "From one vessel to another, may it serve to guard our lands and our people. Let it be done." The chamber tightened around them, and then the pressure broke like a wave, leaving the air sharp and clean.

As Bremusa's voice fell silent, her silver eyes closed, signaling for everyone in the chamber to do the same. The wind inside picked up again, swirling around them as though they were at the center of a vortex. Aurelia straightened her back, her heart rate quickening with every moment that chaos reigned within the stone walls. For several seconds, panic built in her chest, making her feel as if the storm would never end. Just when she was ready to scream for it to stop, the wind stilled, and the chamber grew nearly silent.

A subtle pressure squeezed her left hand, indicating that it was safe to peek. However, Aurelia hesitated, scared of what she might see. When she finally opened her eyes, the portal came to life before them, swirling with colors and creating a vivid window into a world she recognized—one she had missed for so long.

Moving beside Aurelia and taking Bremusa's place, Septima's gaze fixed on the figures materializing within the portal. "Is that...?"

Aurelia gasped, her hand rising to cover her mouth as tears filled her eyes. "Mother." Joy cut as deep as grief. Aurelia felt an overwhelming urge to run, yet she couldn't move at all.

If only there had been one figure on the other side of the window—if there hadn't been so many others she knew in her heart to be alive—she might have thought she was looking at the veil. But unlike the swirling black vortex she and Bremusa had sent Cyrena into, she was staring at the vibrant colors of another world, a living world.

As Septima and Aurelia held hands, tears streaming down both their faces while they stared unblinking at Aurelia's reflection on the portal's surface, their mother—Aurelia's by blood and Septima's by choice—stepped forward through the shimmering gateway. Her fiery red hair framed her ageless face. Behind her followed their father, Proteus, their brother, Amadeus, Variel, and a dozen Norithaean and Aegrician warriors, all appearing weary but alive.

"Impossible," Otera whispered at Aurelia's side, placing a hand on her niece's shoulder.

The weight of the revelation was almost too much to bear, sending Aurelia's heart into a rapid beat that drowned out every other sound around her. Her legs faltered beneath her, and she collapsed to the cave floor, with Septima following suit. The world around her spun as she tried to make sense of the impossible sight before her: their mother, Messalina, the woman she had thought lost forever, was crossing the portal into Ekotoria with her father and brother, both of whom had lived in the human realm their entire lives, escorted by a cadre of Norithaean and Aegrician warriors. A giggle burst from Aurelia's throat as she locked eyes with Variel, not surprised at all that the oracle had managed to bring her family back to her.

"How?" Aurelia choked out, her voice trembling with emotion. The resemblance between her and her mother was striking. Yet, there was a strength in Messalina's eyes that Aurelia had only just begun to find within herself.

Stepping the rest of the way into the chamber, Messalina opened her arms and pulled both her daughters into a hug, with their father and brother enclosing them in their embrace.

Proteus's callused hand trembled against Aurelia's back, and the small, human imperfection undid her.

"Later, my love. For now, let us just be grateful that fate has brought us together again." Gratitude filled the room, but fate seldom stopped at mercy; it always asked for something in return.

Chapter Twenty-Eight

Aurelia
Four Months Later

The soft glow of moonlight filtered through the delicate white curtains, and the open window allowed the gentle sea breeze to flutter the gauzy fabric. Aurelia and Cristos carefully unfolded soft linens and placed them in the corners of the exquisite crib that Otera had gifted them. It was specially made from pine, featuring phoenixes engraved along the sides and gold leaf flames adorning the posts—a stunning piece of Aegrician craftsmanship. The scent of pine mingled with the sea air, creating a fragrance that blessed the cradle with both the strength of the earth and the calm of the ocean. The symbols represented the rebirth and renewal that had come into their lives so many times since they met.

As Cristos leaned down to tuck in the edges of the blanket, his arm brushed against Aurelia's swollen belly, prompting the baby to kick from within, making her gasp. It was a reminder that life stirred inside her, even as the world outside their chamber bore scars of war. Over the past several weeks, their little bundle had become increasingly active.

"Are you alright, my love?" Cristos asked, turning to face her. His cerulean eyes were filled with concern, undoubtedly thinking that it might be time. The healer had said the baby could arrive at any moment, so they were doing their best to prepare. Although they had plenty of people in the palace who could assist in setting up the bed or organizing the baby's clothes, they often wanted to take care of those tasks themselves.

Rising on her toes to kiss him, Aurelia smiled. "Yes, I'm fine. Our little one is just restless tonight."

His lips curved into a smile as he placed his hand on her belly, the child responding with another kick.

For a moment, they stood there, gazing at the crib while Cristos held Aurelia close, one hand resting on her abdomen.

"It's perfect, and having my mother back... my father, brother, and sister here with us... It's just perfect. If only your family could be here as well." Even as her heart swelled with so much love, she thought it would burst, joy and grief intertwined; love often arrived with its shadows. Discovering that her mother was alive and spending the past four months with both her found and blood family had felt like a dream—a real dream that she was able to experience as a person, not a spirit. With her father and brother settling in Ekotoria for good, their family could focus on healing and building the relationships they all deserved. But Cristos' parents were gone, and she knew it pained him. "I can't believe we're going to be parents soon. It's surreal."

"My parents are with us in spirit." Cristos kissed the top of her head, his voice carrying a tender note of awe that resonated deep within her soul. "After everything, we will finally have our family together. We'll be able to raise our child in peace."

Peace. For so long, it seemed as though peace would never touch their shores, but with their enemies defeated and the portal restored, Ekotoria had become calm. Unshed tears blurred Aurelia's vision as she processed this thought.

"I couldn't have done any of this without you and our friends. Our kingdoms are stronger because we stand side by side."

***

Finished setting up the crib so it would be ready for when their child made its debut, Aurelia and Cristos headed back into their bedchamber. Candlelight flickered in the moonlit darkness, chasing away shadows and creating a peaceful ambiance in the room.

"Come, my love." With his hand on the small of her back, Cristos guided her to their spacious bed, helping her to climb up. "You deserve some rest." Rest had become rare and precious, a treasure as necessary as steel had once been.

Pushing herself up on the bed, she curled her finger at him in a come-hither motion. "Only if you join me."

She didn't have to ask twice. Without a moment of hesitation, he slid onto the bed beside and patted the mattress beside him. The back rubs had become their nightly ritual, one she would miss once the baby was born.

Sliding off her sleeping gown, she rolled onto her side next to him, his strong hands finding the tense knots in her shoulders. She sighed as her body melted into the mattress under his fingers, every muscle relaxing one by one. "Your touch is like magic."

"Anything for you, my queen," Cristos whispered, pressing a tender kiss to the nape of her neck.

Aurelia's breath caught in her chest, a shiver of desire cascading down her spine. Even though her body was swollen and tired, he still found a way to make her body sing, and desire made her feel more alive than fear ever had. The more he touched her, the more she wanted him.

Rolling over onto her back, she slid her hand around his back, pulling his mouth to hers, the passion of his kiss leaving her breathless. Their tongues entwined, teasing and tasting each other, igniting the fire within Aurelia. His hands cupped her cheek, tipping her head and deepening the kiss. Moaning softly, she arched into him, her body desperate for more of his touch.

Knowing how sensitive her body was, his fingers trailed down her neck, over her collarbone, and then lower, tracing the curve of her breasts that had become so much fuller over the past weeks. She gasped, her nipple hardening under his touch, which only encouraged him to wrap his lips around the tight bud. His fingers found the delicate fabric of her undergarments and, with a soft tug, slipped them off her body.

"You're so exquisite like this," he whispered against her skin, his voice husky with desire.

Every cell in her body was on fire, his words only heating her more. "Please, Cristos... I need you."

When her fingers threaded into his thick hair and gently guided his head to move down between her thighs, he didn't hesitate. Sliding down her body, his tongue trailed a teasing path along her inner thigh before reaching the source of her heat.

"What do you need, my queen?"

He knew the answer to the question, and she was beyond words, only gasps leaving her lips as the ghost of his warm breath skittered across her most sensitive parts.

With the first swipe of his tongue, Aurelia's mind went blank, every thought replaced by the intense pleasure coursing through her body. She gasped, her fingers tangling in his hair as he continued to explore her. Each flick of his tongue sent shivers up her spine, drawing her closer to the edge. Her breathing grew ragged, her chest heaving, and the world around her shattered as ecstasy overwhelmed her, wave after wave of pleasure crashing through her body until she was left trembling beneath him.

Wordlessly, he positioned himself above her, his throbbing cock poised at her entrance. "Is this what you want?"

All she managed was a nod before he guided himself inside her, stretching her body around him deliciously.

Hooking one leg over his shoulder, he began to move, his hips rocking with a steady rhythm as he buried himself deep within her. Aurelia wrapped one hand around his thigh, loving how his muscles flexed beneath her fingertips.

"Ah, gods...Aurelia." His pace quickened, the friction sending shockwaves of pleasure coursing through her.

"Harder, Cristos," she urged, her nails digging into his back. The pressure building inside her was unbearable.

Cristos obliged, his thrusts coming deeper and faster, his wings flaring out behind him as he seemed to lose himself in the intensity. The world around them seemed to melt away, leaving only the two of them. She gripped his thighs harder, pulling him deep into her core, wanting to feel every inch of him.

Finally, the dam broke, and Aurelia cried out, her body clenching around him as her climax sent her into pure ecstasy. With a deep moan, his body shuddered as he rode through his own orgasm.

Spent and breathless, he collapsed beside her, pulling her close as they tried to catch their breath. As they lay there, tangled in each other's arms, Aurelia knew it was only the beginning of their life together, and that brought a smile to her face as she drifted off to sleep, knowing her dreams that night would be happy ones. Outside, the sea kept its rhythm, steady as the breath of a kingdom finally at peace.

The sun rose above the horizon three days later, its rays reflecting the tension coiled within Aurelia's entire being. She lay on the bed, sweat pouring down her face as she panted through another contraction, each one more powerful than the last. The chamber felt smaller with every wave of pain, time itself bending around her struggle.

"Almost there, my love," Cristos murmured, his voice a soothing balm against the searing pain tearing through her body as he held her hand tightly.

"Can you... Can you see the baby yet?" Aurelia gasped between labored breaths, her heart thundering in her chest as fear and anticipation warred within her.

"Very soon," her mother reassured her, standing beside the healer, Cordelia, who was providing assistance. "You're doing so well, little bird."

"Remember, deep breaths," Cordelia advised, checking Aurelia's progress while bracing her hand on Aurelia's knee.

"If it's a girl, her name will be Calliope," Aurelia whispered, tears streaming down her cheeks as another contraction surged through her.

Leaning forward, Cristos kissed her on the forehead. "It's a beautiful name. I love it."

Her mother stepped closer, taking Aurelia's other hand. "It's after my mother, who was taken too soon." She smiled gently, brushing Aurelia's crimson hair off her sweaty forehead. "She would be very proud."

"Push, Aurelia!" Cordelia urged, reaching for the clean towel in Septima's hands. "Your baby is almost here." The command rang out like a battle cry, but this was the fiercest fight of her life.

With a guttural cry, Aurelia summoned every last ounce of strength from her exhausted body and pushed. The world around her blurred into nothingness as she focused on bringing their precious child into the world.

"Here they come!" Eyes glassy with emotion, Septima placed her hand on Aurelia's knee. "You're doing so well, sissy!"

In mere moments, the pressure in Aurelia's lower body turned into the worst pain she had ever experienced, but then it eased as their child entered the world.

"It's a girl!" Cordelia exclaimed, pulling the baby close in a towel and beginning to clean her.

Tiny wails filled the room as Aurelia collapsed back onto the bed, her body wracked with exhaustion but her heart over-flowing with love. Beside her, Cristos still held her hand, his glassy eyes unable to look away from his daughter, especially as the healer placed the tiny bundle in his arms.

"Meet her, my love," he said, leaning down to place the child on Aurelia's chest. "Meet Calliope." Aurelia traced the tiny hand with her fingertip, wonder eclipsing every scar of the past.

Days later, the kingdom prepared to welcome its newest princess. As the sun rose, bathing the palace in golden light,

Aurelia cradled Calliope in her arms, feeling a fierce protectiveness and love that she had never experienced before.

Together, she and Cristos stepped out onto their balcony, with their stunning blue-eyed baby in Cristos' arms. Calliope's tuft of crimson hair caught the sunlight beautifully. The crowd's roar rose like a tide, washing away every doubt Aurelia had ever known.

"Today, we introduce our daughter, Calliope, to her people," Cristos said, smiling down at Aurelia with a joy that only true love can bring.

Aurelia gently touched their baby's cheek before gazing around at the scene. Behind them on the balcony stood their family—both biological and chosen—including Aurelia's mother, father, sister, and brother. Three of them were people she never thought she would see again until that fateful night in the caves. Supported by their presence, she recalled the prophecy spoken to her mother before her own birth and made a promise to her kingdom: "She will be a symbol of hope, unity, and strength for our kingdom as we usher in a new age of peace." And although she knew that peace was as fragile as glass, she also understood that hope was the fire that reforged it.

Chapter Twenty-Nine

Kason

Five Months Later

Kason cradled their newborn son, Kyro, gazing at the tiny sleeping face nestled against his chest. The baby's soft tufts of silver hair caught the gentle light filtering through the cottage window, casting a warm glow on his smooth cheeks. Kason's heart beat slower, steadier, as if the world itself had paused to honor the small miracle in his arms. He marveled at the delicate perfection of his child, tracing the curve of the little one's lips with his thumb.

When he glanced back up at the bed, he met stunning violet eyes watching him, with Holera's silver hair shimmering in the dim glow of the fire. Having only given birth a few days earlier, she was still recovering. They had sent the healer back to Flamecliff. Still, his mate was nowhere near ready to resume her usual activities, no matter how stubborn she was. Even in her weakened state, she radiated strength, her spirit too wild to be confined by rest. If it were up to Holera, she would already be soaring through the skies or practicing her already expert-level skills with her bow.

Leaving the warmth of the fire at his back, Kason crossed the room to where she rested, sitting on the edge of the bed.

"He's perfect, my fierce warrior. Just like you." The words were simple, but within them lived every vow he had ever made to her.

Holera smiled, her gaze softening as she reached out to gently stroke their baby's cheek. "I don't know about me being perfect, but he definitely is. I can't believe he's finally here, and that we created this beautiful child together." Her voice held both disbelief and reverence, as if motherhood were a gift she had stolen from the stars.

The warmth of love exploded in Kason's chest as his gaze shifted from the child in his arms, who was a perfect blend of both of them, to his mate. The sight of them together filled him with a fiercer devotion than any battle ever had. "Indeed, we did... even if magical coral made it happen."

The sun dipped just behind the Aegrician mountains as Holera shifted out of her phoenix form in front of her mother's cottage just outside Flamecliff. Kason stood by her side, holding their one-month-old son in his arms. Excitement bubbled in his chest at the thought of introducing their little bundle to their friends and to Holera's mother, Aura. They had traveled to Flamecliff for a special occasion, but they only had one night to spend in Aura's cottage before heading to the palace. The path smelled of pine and hearth smoke, each breath steeped in memory and homecoming.

"Ready?" Holera asked, adjusting her cloak, her silver hair brilliant against the dark fabric. Against Kason's chest, their baby slept soundly, wrapped in a blanket to keep him warm in the cool mountain air.

Nodding, Kason followed her to the front door, but before Holera had a chance to knock, the door creaked open. Aura's face lit up like the first rays of morning sun as she opened the door wider to welcome them inside.

"Holera! Kason!"

Kason's grin widened as he uncovered their child and held him up toward his grandmother. Aura's violet eyes sparkled even more. They hadn't seen the matriarch for months, so while she knew her daughter was pregnant, she hadn't yet met their child. "And this is Kyro... your grandson."

"A boy?" Aura reached out, brushing her fingers across the baby's soft cheek. "Hello, little one." Her words seemed to wrap the child in generations of love, binding the past to the future with nothing more than a whisper. Pure awe and love filled Aura's voice as she gazed down at the baby, whose tuft of silver hair matched her own. As Kyro opened his vibrant green eyes, he gripped his grandmother's finger, eliciting a laugh from her. "Oh, you're going to be a strong boy, just like your father."

The pride in Kason's chest burned even brighter at the compliment, but he couldn't take the credit. "He's going to be strong like his mother," he said, placing Kyro in Aura's outstretched arms. "Not even my strength can compare to her fire." His voice held quiet pride, not in himself, but in the fierce, un-yielding woman he was blessed to call his mate.

Chapter Thirty

Otera

Under a canopy of intertwining branches in the palace gardens, Otera and Blaedia stood before Bremusa, a surge of unwavering love coursing through Otera's veins. Their loved ones encircled them, but it was Otera's sister, Messalina, who stood just to her left that brought tears to her eyes as she prepared to commit herself to Blaedia for eternity. Otera had believed Messalina to be dead for more than a decade. Her sister's silent support during this crucial moment meant the world to her. The garden's blossoms seemed to blur as if even the flowers wept at the sight of love reclaimed.

"Otera and Blaedia," Bremusa began, her silver eyes nearly white in the sunlight. "You have chosen to unite your lives, to merge your destinies, and face whatever challenges life may bring together."

As she spoke, Otera's heartbeat thrummed in her ears, yet her hand remained steady as she clasped Blaedia's—her mate for decades and the love of her life.

With a ceremonial dagger in hand, Bremusa extended it to them. "Give me your hands."

Having attended many Aegrician weddings in her life, Otera understood why Bremusa wanted their hands and happily placed hers into Bremusa's, feeling relief wash over her when Blaedia did the same.

"Blood is life," Bremusa said, making a shallow cut across each of their palms. "And from this moment on, you will be joined by the very essence of your beings."

Crimson beads welled up, yet neither flinched. Instead, they gazed into each other's eyes as Bremusa turned their palms together and wrapped their hands in a white cloth. The cloth absorbed their mingled blood, symbolizing a bond that would outlast crowns and kingdoms.

"Our kingdom has witnessed your fierce dedication to one another and how your love has grown since you chose each other as mates so long ago. By connecting yourselves through marriage, you demonstrate to each other—and your people—just how deeply you love one another. As your blood flows together, you become one. No matter where you go from here, you will always be a part of each other."

Tears burned in the back of Otera's eyes as she looked up at the woman she adored—the one who had never given up on finding her when she had been taken, and who had never left her side since her return.

With her free hand, Blaedia stroked Otera's cheek, wiping away her tears. "You are everything to me, my fires, and I cannot wait to see what fate has in store for us." Her words were as steady as steel yet warm as flame—a promise no storm could undo.

As the sun dipped toward the horizon, Otera and Blaedia's reception was in full swing in the palace gardens, with laughter and music filling the night air.

Otera scanned the crowd, her heart brimming with joy. Once, it had been a tomb of grief; now it beat like a drum of celebration. Surrounded by love and even new life among her friends, the scene stood in stark contrast to a year prior, when their entire continent had been brought to its knees by the barbarians from the south. Just a few feet away, Cristos and Kason held their babies, laughing about something Otera couldn't hear. The sound—simple and full of life—was more triumphant than any war cry. Even her commander, Taryn, who had died in the war and been brought back to life, had found true love; she rested a hand on her slightly swollen belly while Lars whispered sweetly in her ear.

In the middle of the dance floor, Septima danced with her father, while Aurelia twirled with her brother. Messalina looked on, her big blue eyes shining with pure happiness as she watched over her family. The circle of family, once shattered, felt whole again beneath the lantern glow.

"Look at them all," Otera whispered to her new wife, gesturing toward the crowd. "Have you ever seen such a happy sight?"

A grin spread across Blaedia's lips as she leaned in and kissed Otera softly, lingering just long enough to send a shiver down Otera's spine. "Love is powerful enough to overcome any evil, my fires."

Near the center of the dance floor, Exie, who had already enjoyed several glasses of whiskey, let out a whoop and transformed into her brilliantly colored phoenix form in a burst of fire, launching herself into the air. Moments later, Aurelia's crimson wings erupted from her back, and she followed Holera as they ascended. Blaedia placed another kiss on Otera's lips before stepping away, a mischievous glint in her eyes. Even in matrimony, she remained the fire Otera had fallen in love with—untamed, radiant, eternal. "I'll be right back!"

In flames that rivaled those of the garden's central fire, Blaedia's crimson and black phoenix form shot into the sky behind her friends.

The air crackled with energy as the phoenixes soared, their vibrant feathers shimmering in the sunset—each one unique yet beautiful. Otera stood among those she loved, watching as the phoenixes danced through the sky, their joyous calls echoing all around her. Her heart swelled with pride for all they had accomplished and hope for the future generations of Aegricia. It was a new chapter, filled with light and love, and she could hardly wait to see what wonders it would bring. As the phoenixes carved trails of fire into the twilight, Otera realized that the prophecy had not only been fulfilled; it had blossomed into something even greater: a legacy of love strong enough to light every dawn to come.

Epilogue

The crackle of fire filled the great hall of the palace, with flames dancing across the carved stone like golden feathers. Outside, the night was cold and silent, but within these walls, laughter warmed the air.

Aurelia sat with Calliope in her arms, the infant's crimson hair glinting in the firelight. Beside her, Cristos leaned close, his wing wrapped around them like a living shield. Across from them, Holera and Kason watched as Kyro's tiny fists clenched in the air, the babe safely nestled in Holera's embrace. Kason grinned, his eyes shining with a joy fiercer than any victory on the battlefield.

On the other side of the hearth, Otera rested her head against Blaedia's shoulder, their hands entwined, wedding bands glinting softly. For once, the queen-turned-matriarch felt no burden pressing down on her. Her blue eyes softened as she watched the younger generation—her niece, her family—experiencing the peace she had once feared they would never know.

Messalina sat nearby with Proteus at her side, their hands clasped tightly as if afraid to let go again after so many years apart. Amadeus lounged close by, teasing Septima as though no time had ever separated their family. For Aurelia, seeing

them all together—both blood relatives and found family—felt more miraculous than any prophecy fulfilled.

Exie snorted into her whiskey, making Septima laugh from her seat nearby. Even Taryn, her hand resting protectively over her swelling belly, rolled her eyes fondly as Lars tucked a blanket around her shoulders.

The fire popped, sending sparks toward the high-vaulted ceiling. In the quiet that followed, Aurelia glanced around at everyone, her heart so full it ached. "The prophecy brought us here," she said softly, "but love... love is what will carry us forward."

No one argued, for no one needed to. The flames glowed brighter, reflected in every gaze, and in that moment, the future felt certain: whatever challenges lay ahead, they would face them together.

The End.

ENJOYED CROWN OF THE PROPHECY?

If you enjoyed Crown of the Prophecy, please leave a review!
https://buy.bookfunnel.com/ep0pppikqh
While Crown of the Phoenix series is a trilogy, there are multiple other books connected to the series, such as Mate of the Phoenix and Shadowed by Prophecy, as well as others to come!
Sign up for C. A. Varian's newsletter to receive current updates on her new and upcoming releases, sales, and giveaways:
https://sendfox.com/cavarian
You can also find all stories, books, and social media pages and follow her here:
https://cavarian.com/

Also by C.A. Varian

Crown of the Phoenix Series
Crown of the Phoenix
Crown of the Exiled
Crown of the Prophecy
Mate of the Phoenix
Shadowed by Prophecy
Shadowed by the Veil (Coming Soon)

My Alien Mate Series
My Alien Protector
My Alien Rescuer (coming soon!)

Other World Series
The Other World
The Other Key
The Other Fate

Hazel Watson Mystery Series
Kindred Spirits: Prequel
The Sapphire Necklace
Justice for the Slain
Whispers from the Swamp
Crossroads of Darkness
The Spirit Collector

The Darkness that Follows (Coming Soon)

The Cursed Waters Duet
Song of Death
Goddess of Death

Survivor & Savior Duet
Saving Scarlett
Keeping Caroline

Standalones
Second Chance with Santa
When Everly Saved Emerald Hollow (Coming Soon with A.A. Weaver)
Spirit of the Dying Flower
The Gladiatrix & the Fallen Son (Coming Soon)
Wings of the Forgotten (Coming Soon with J. Paige)

Acknowledgements

This book would not exist without the people who carried me when I couldn't carry it alone.

To my amazing Executive Assistant, Jessica, thank you for helping me keep my head on straight. You make it possible for me to keep this thing going.

To my incredible PA, Aly Dust, thank you for being a creative force and a constant source of support.

To my awesome editor, Willow Oak Author Services, thank you for keeping up with my crazy schedule.

To my super supportive Street Team, your enthusiasm, love, and loyalty made all the difference. You were the wind at my back through every draft.

To my husband, children, and family, thank you for your patience, love, and for understanding that writing a book means sometimes living in another world.

To my readers, thank you for returning to the page, for believing in haunted girls and broken curses, and for holding space in your hearts for stories like this.

Thank you to my cover designers, Artisan Gallery and Artscandare, as well as D'Arte Oriel, for the awesome chapter header design.

From the bottom of my heart, thank you.

XOXO, Cherie

About the Author

Born and raised in the heart of Louisiana's Cajun Country, I'm a passionate writer of dark, fantasy, paranormal, and even alien romances—if there's a romance involved, chances are I've written it. My stories are filled with mystery, magic, and intense emotional connections that keep readers on the edge of their seats.

When I'm not writing, you'll find me creating special editions of my books packed with all the bells and whistles—character art, exclusive swag, and more for my readers to treasure. I love connecting with fans, whether it's through my TikTok shop, my website, or in person at events where I can share the stories I pour my heart into.

proud mother and new grandmother, I've faced many challenges in life, including a battle with chronic Lyme disease, but I've never let it define me. Writing is my escape and my passion, and with the support of my amazing assistant Jessica, my husband Trevor, and my daughters, Arianna and Brianna, I'm living my dream of writing full-time. Even my two youngest sisters pitch in, helping me with various tasks for the business—it's truly a family affair!

At home in the coastal region of Mississippi, surrounded by love, laughter, and inspiration, I'm never without my two Shih Tzus, Charlie and Luna, along with my three mischievous cats—Ramses, Simba, and Cookie. Whether I'm doting on my furry companions, reading, or soaking up family time, every moment is a precious one.

Join me as I continue to create worlds full of romance, adventure, and unforgettable characters that you won't want to put down!